Sean F Campbell

JUDGE

First published 2019.

Cover artwork and design by David Mallows.

To Mum

— Your enduring support and encouragement finally got me to put pen to paper.

To Katie

— My light in the black, you vanquished the demons of self doubt and spurred me on to finish this.

To Tina

— Walks with you are when my mind wanders best.

ONE

THAT CONSTANT DIN of the news again: a type of dirge that can only come from a lengthy chorus of bad news. A fatal shooting on Scotland Road, a stabbing outside a bar in Anfield, a Polish immigrant racially abused on the train – all of that was enough to make even the happiest person feel down, *despite* the token-happy-ending final story about a cat that fell five stories and managed to remain alive and well.

Linda didn't take much notice of it though: safe in her semi-detached home in Crosby, she didn't have a care in the world as she finished dusting the living room. Her boy, Benny, was at school. His tea would be ready soon for when he came in at 4pm, full of beans and 'starving' like all eight-year-olds will often claim to be after two or so hours without food. Mick, her husband, was at work driving forklifts for a car manufacturing plant. He was on day shifts this week and wouldn't be back until midnight. She missed his company during the long, 12-hour days – but he was well-paid, and that meant she could be the stay-at-home housewife that she had always wanted to be.

With an emphatic press of the large red button on the remote, Linda forced the vibrant colours of the high-definition screen to a dull, lifeless charcoal. A drama documentary about serial killers had been about to start.

She hated such programmes as they were always so dreary. With the spate of gory killings that had recently been plaguing the country, anything about murders was especially unwelcome right now. Person or persons unknown were committing grizzly acts of torture on some deeply unfortunate individuals from all walks of life. Police had stated on numerous occasions that they did not believe the victims to be linked, but more recently, they were investigating the possible theory of a Manson-esque gang. Linda would not be surprised if this was the case: she blamed the internet for creating all manner of perversions and for allowing sick individuals to indulge in their personal fetishes without consequence, and it was as a matter of when, rather than if, something as dark as this would come of it.

The pervasive silence made the house feel bleak, almost unnerving, so Linda switched the radio on. Though she did not drive much, Linda liked the presenter on the afternoon show on the local station, 'Merseytalk.' She almost jumped out of her skin when the heavy guitar riff shot out of the speakers. Mick loved rock music: it was one of the few things they did not have in common, and right there and then, Eric Clapton's 'Layla' was by no means welcome – in fact, it never had been, and she always made her husband turn such music down or off. Linda had never really been a fan of rock music, or much music in general – 80s pop was about as far as she cared to adventure. With the station changed, Linda made a cup of tea and stretched out on the sofa, awaiting whatever that day's 'hot topic' was going to be.

TWO

Turning off the murder documentary had proved to be in vain.

"Just when the country had started to calm down, another vile murder has gripped the British public."

A northern accent introduced the main story and Linda had to check that she hadn't put the national news on by mistake. Merseytalk was usually about local issues, like church closures, supermarket planning permits and football banter.

"The body of a man has been found in New Brighton. It is believed to have been dumped on the beach during the early hours of this morning. This latest atrocity falls into the same category as those which have been going on nationwide: brutal torture, resulting in eventual death."

Linda was horrified: it was all too easy to remain concerned-yet-comfortable when bad news is not on the doorstep and lacks any personal connection; she was not at all comfortable having heard this breaking news.

"Sensitive listeners, please be advised: graphic descriptions are ahead. The victim is believed to have had several body parts severed and their eyes removed. An initial police state-ment suggests that there are signs of restraints on the wrists and legs, but full details will be revealed following the autopsy report. This latest victim is believed to be in his mid 40s and is said to be a government employee."

The phone lines would soon be open for listeners to discuss the issue, but the room was plunged into silence before the usually smooth presenter, who now had a slight tremor in his voice as he made his opening greeting, could announce their opening.

The murder had been and gone but Linda was left feeling substantially uncomfortable and the unlikelihood of lightening striking twice could not put her mind at ease. As far as Linda was concerned, she had never done anything to hurt anyone; she saw herself as someone who was always nice and pleasant to people. This apparent cult seemed to pick people completely at random, and she was frightened at the idea that she could be next. That plummeting feeling that comes with both a great fall and a nauseating bout of nervousness suddenly assaulted her stomach. The half cup of tea that was still left in her mug lost its appeal at about the same time that the G-Plan sofa lost any semblance of its usually-unquestionable comfort. Linda picked up her keys and walked out to her olive-green Ford Focus. An early trip to pick up Benny was on the cards.

THREE

Hot and tired, as well as both physically and mentally exhausted after what he would later deem a swine of a day, a large brute of a man kicked off his shoes and collapsed on his sofa. Blood, sweat and tears had been the case at work, and he had certainly earned his corn today. Some people believed that judges had it easy, but this one did not – *most certainly not.*

Roger Birch put full effort into every day. Passing a sentence on people was not easy – *by no means easy at all.* Judge Birch relied on hard evidence, *he* needed to be convinced. He held the firm belief that a person could be made to put their hand on a bible and swear to tell the truth, but to save their own skin or the life of a friend, even the most devout man would tell a few white lies – maybe even weave a complex web of deceit with one monster of a lie at the centre. Witnesses could *not* be trusted as far as Judge Birch was concerned. Why their testimonies should lessen the sentence for some villain was a mystery best left for judges from more privileged backgrounds to trouble themselves with.

Judge Birch was taking longer to recover from each court session and get his head back together. That day's defendant was a former job centre employee who had caused a lot of harm to a lot of people by using the powers the state gave him in a most irresponsible way. Roger hated people like this, those who prey upon folk in bleak situations who were most in need of help. David Goldstein had gone a bit crazy when Roger passed the sentence: he had needed additional restraint. Judge Birch knew that some may think the sentence he dealt unfair, but the punishment, as far as he was concerned, should fit the crime – and sentencing guidelines had become a farce, anyway. Predators like him were were worthy of the heftiest sentence he could pass: *a hefty sentence indeed.*

Roger opened a bottle of supermarket bourbon whiskey, 'Rebel Fire.' It was neither Jack Daniel's nor Jim Beam, but it tasted good value for money at £10.99. His main reason for purchasing it: he thought that the name sounded a little like a Lynyrd Skynyrd song. Taking a big glug straight from the bottle, Roger swallowed hard and dropped onto his sofa. He didn't enjoy his work and was looking forward to retirement. He would preside over a few more cases, and then he would ditch the robes and wig for a more peaceful life.

After a few more slugs, which depleted the bottle by about a third, Roger got up and looked out at the glistening lights across the River Mersey. There was a lot of cloud and not a star in sight. He loved the stars, but the sparkle in his life had long-since dulled and, despite having a flat with a view that folk would pay a sizeable sum to enjoy from their living room window, Roger often felt that he had become blind to that which was beautiful in life. His work had taken too much out of him, and life in general had hauled his mind against the coals of a harsh reality. What was done could not be undone, but he was intent on getting things in order and making the best of it in whatever way he could.

A tight fist dragged the curtains closed one at a time, despite the efforts of the rusty rail which fought against doing the very purpose for which it was created – if it ever did it in the first place: *who in God's name made curtain rails like this anyway?* The city lights were nice, but he left them in the living room: he needed darkness to sleep. Roger threw himself onto the bed, casting his hands behind his head in the fashion of someone who is more angry than tired.

The light passing under the bedroom door suggested the living room was not illuminated by the city lights alone. Whether he had forgotten to turn off the lamp or if it was just that he was beyond caring about the electricity bill anymore was a question that Roger found himself unable to answer. Live to work or work to live: it was all merging into one lately. Roger closed his eyes in the hope of escaping into sleep and drifted away on the thought that he would be glad when it was all over.

FOUR

Linda had spent the morning watching the local news: as usual, it focused on the previous days' big event. It was always the same with news: a celebrity dies, a new craze catches on, a natural disaster occurs. Whatever it was, it always regurgitated for roughly a week, sometimes a fortnight, until everyone got sick of it and found something else to take an interest in. Linda had remembered the disappearance of Flight 370, the Jimmy Saville fiasco and even Madeleine McCann's abduction – which Linda continued to take delight in deeming 'absolute hogwash' to anyone who would listen. Such stories provoked great sympathy for those involved and suffering, at first, but even the most empathetic individual will admit that a truly heart-wrenching story can become tedious if repeated day-after-day, with the only difference being a fresh news reporter or a sound-bite from a neighbour who enjoys their five minutes of fame.

It had been a long time since a spree of murders had been the focus, and Linda thought it farcical that in 2015 – in the age of DNA – police could not seem to draw any conclusions: *an absolute farce if ever there was one*. All these thoughts and the news in general had been plaguing Linda's mind the entire morning as it repeated itself; nonetheless, she found herself unable to turn it off with the gruesome event occurring so close to home.

Without realising, Linda had mimicked the repetition of the news as Mick was forced to endure her ramblings and speculations throughout the entire night; the last thing he needed after returning home following a gruelling 12-hour shift. It was an unusually cold November, and being sat immobile in a forklift truck for most of the day wasn't ideal for maintaining a decent body temperature: even thick gloves and extra socks did not ease Mick's shivering throughout his shift. Linda would have happily rabbited on the entire night, but Mick finally found salvation from his wife's bleating: he fell asleep as soon as his head hit the pillow, such was his state of fatigue.

Their son, Benny, had proved great respite for Linda. Her time with him helped occupy her mind, and she focused less on her current woes. His favourite CD of 'Happy, Wacky Farm' had been on repeat when she took him to school. Normally one play of the track is more than most parents could handle, but today he was overjoyed to have his Mum play it *seven* times on the car journey to school. It was a silly song and probably aimed at younger children, but he enjoyed it all the same. She hated dropping him off and even played the CD herself on the way home so as to avoid the silence. The temptation to turn on the radio news reared its ugly head as the hour-mark passed; the dial beckoned her to flood her mind with the latest updates – updates that could either abate fears by informing that the killer was arrested or feed them by stating that they were believed to be even nearer.

As noon approached, Linda was stood in the kitchen and a dog-tired Mick had emerged from their bedroom, grudgingly gearing up for another 12-hour stint in the cold. He threw 6 spoons of 'Jet Fuel' coffee into a large plastic jug usually reserved for mixing instant gravy and sauces. He then added half boiling and half cold water, before giving it a vigorous stir and downing it in one. His grimace signified the foul and bitter taste of the beverage, but he was drinking it more to make a point that his wife's over-the-top moaning was not welcome – *certainly not* in the precious few hours he was able to reserve for sleep.

Mick was a caring husband: not as loving as when they'd first met, but he was always nice to his wife even though his job had been knocking the stuffing out of his spirit lately. Without even checking if she was watching the television, he turned the news off that his wife was fixating on and changed the channel to football news. There were some big games coming up this weekend and Mick had a five-team accumulator bet that he kept referring to as a 'gift from God' due to the odds being so long for events that Mick regarded as 'dead certs.' Linda offered him breakfast in a brusque tone, but he said he would get something at work: he hated falseness and was not someone who would accept niceties from someone unless they were sincere. Linda knew her husband hated the vending machine junk that was on offer at the factory, and it was blindingly obvious to her that he was making a point of sulking – something she despised him doing. The outside world may have viewed them as a relatively pleasant and happy couple, but in recent times she had found herself increasingly detesting her husband on an alarming number of occasions.

As Mick sat glued to the television, Linda reminisced. Her life was not so hard now compared to how it used to be as a disability assessor for the government. The recession had proved to be a Pandora's Box which conjured up all manner of government cut backs. Many areas had faced harsh cuts since the global financial crisis began, but Whitehall's latest hard-on was for those claiming disability benefits to be re-evaluated. The old, the immobile, the infirm – and many more groups of unfortunate individuals – found themselves facing the wrath of the government's scythe.

Numerous cases had hit the front pages: people stepping out whilst needlessly clutching a walking stick, others going jogging despite telling previous assessors they had serious chest issues. Linda's job was to decide who was faking and who was worthy, but as with almost every modern-day job, she had strict targets from her managers. At first, she tried to be nice. She would pass almost anyone, as long as they looked mildly pitiful or told a sob story well. As target figures grew stricter, those passes soon earned her a strong warning from her bosses.

"Don't you realise these people are playing you for an idiot? Less than 25% of these bums are legitimately eligible for disability benefit; the rest can either go and get a job or do the world a favour and drop dead. We've got targets, Linda: hit them or you're out!"

It was a defining statement for Linda. She was sure

that the rant of her superior was carried out with the purpose of firing her up to hit targets, but she wondered, in the back of her mind, if she really was getting taken for a ride by the people walking into her office. She started to imagine them walking away, stifling a laugh because she had gone so easy on them. The idea nested itself in the back of her mind and had no intention of leaving.

That was back in 2009: Mick was out of work, and they had a baby boy to take care of. Linda knew that she couldn't afford to lose the job, so she forced herself to become harder – *colder*. She started to sum people up before they'd even opened their mouths, sometimes before she had even seen them. She would look at the forms which they had filled in, which were intended to be "solely for reference purposes," and base her judgement on the slightest of factors – such as neat handwriting: she viewed it as a sign of someone of strength and in good health, not of an individual with a disability. Linda turned one or two claimants down purely because she did not like their names; she pushed her conscience to one side by telling herself that, if they *truly* wanted and *deserved* the benefit, they would appeal. She wasn't going to lose *her* job and have *her* family suffer just because a bunch of 'deadbeats' and 'cretins' needed looking after. Their families or friends should take care of them, not the government. In her small office, tears flowed often and insults were hurled at her. One or two even attempted to assault her, but security were always available at the push of a button.

Linda soon began to smash her targets, a fact

which earned her heaps of praise from her bosses, and even some of the higher-ups sent their congratulations. Bonuses were dished out on a monthly basis and, more often than not, Linda was getting the lion's share of her team's. She was more than aware that she might have let a few genuine folk lose out on their benefit along the way, but soon found ways of not only coping with the guilt but justifying her actions and ridding herself of the nagging-voice-that-was-her-conscience altogether.

Eventually, when Mick got his new job at the car manufacturer, he told Linda he would like her to be a housewife, as he didn't agree with their son being in the care of a nanny just so they could earn more money between them. Linda had come to enjoy her job and thrived on meeting and exceeding the targets she was set whilst raking in the handsome bonuses. She resented Mick's idea at first: she was furious that he even suggested it, but in the end she did what he wanted: not for him but for her Benny. At the reluctance of her supervisor and her own sense of self-determination, she handed in her four-weeks' notice and became the housewife that she had never quite imagined she would be. Though she came to enjoy being a mother to Benny, she always bore a resentment towards Mick for having suggested that she leave her position – had he never suggested she do so, she was doubtful that she ever would have left.

Linda leaned on the breakfast bar and watched the pundits discuss that day's possible match outcomes. Her husband had paid more attention to the odds on his betting slip than he had to her all morning. As far as she was concerned, the man did not care in the slightest that a murder just over the river had left her shaken to the core. He eventually rose and gave her a half-hearted kiss goodbye: he knew it would create an argument if he neglected that too. As nice and innocent as Linda may have appeared to many, Mick knew she had a cold, hard and ruthless streak: the disability assessment officer streak. That job had brought out a side in his wife that he despised. Had he known she had such a streak within her then he may well never have proposed all those years ago. He certainly would not have put a baby in her belly.

That was just the tough luck of life. By the time Mick had realised what his wife was truly capable of, Benny was alive and kicking – and there was no way he was going to play weekend Dad, with a trip to McDonald's being the highlight of his fatherhood. This was how life was – *he just had to accept it and be glad it was not worse.*

FIVE

It was a sunny, winter afternoon. Roger had decided to talk a long walk along the promenade in an effort to clear his head. As a judge, he would often sit and reflect upon his decisions, making certain in his mind that they had been the correct ones – or at least trying to find a way of justifying them. When he would find himself within touching distance of the Holy Grail that was blessed peace of mind, his mind would always find a way of making him feel uncomfortable yet again. He was never able to get both feet off the trap door beneath which beckoned a pit of despair, regret and depression. Roger had not been feeling at ease with much at all in recent times, and a tempest raged inside his head on a daily basis. There were times when he wanted to walk away from it all, but leaving prior to the retirement plan which he had allocated himself would only cause him to be forever shackled by regret. Roger was not going to let that happen – he had a job to do – and forced his mind to erect walls to keep the dark thoughts out where he would stand behind them in his metaphorical fortress and focus on adopting the required persona. *In for a penny, in for a pound.*

A number of seagulls were hovering in the wind, in the way that was often attributed as the inspiration for the design of the Supermarine Spitfire. There weren't many people at the beach. The sun was pleasant but there was an icy bite to the wind. Snow was forecast for the coming days, and experts had predicted a most dire winter for the majority of the United Kingdom. When Roger had heard that news, he gave a pitiful grunt of laughter. As far as he was concerned, his life was bleak enough as it was. Snow, sleet and freezing temperatures were nothing compared to the daily anguish which his mind endured.

There was a car park at each end of the promenade and Roger had parked in the one by the swimming pool with the aim of making the other one, just before the coastal path, his halfway point. There was a small van there which served food and drinks: nothing too fancy, just tea, coffee, chips, burgers and a variety of cakes. Business looked to be almost non-existent for it today with hardly a car in sight, a far cry from the usual hustle and bustle of the summer months. Roger mused to himself how distant a memory summer was to him now. *Distant indeed.*

Roger's chest tightened as he felt a pain within it which was becoming all too frequent. It felt as though an invisible skeletal hand was reaching in and seizing his heart. He pursed his lips to combat the lump in his throat. Grief was like a dark pit and Roger often got that plummeting feeling of falling into it if he let his mind wander to crippling thoughts which he attempted to banish but would not let go of altogether. He sometimes thought that the invisible bony hand would one day reveal the rest of itself and finally the grim reaper would have caught up with him, a large part of Roger knew that if that moment ever occurred, he would welcome it.

"Just a coffee there please, love." Roger was smiling as he handed over the five-pound note. He had a warm smile and the woman at the van returned the gesture. She was glad to see another face – as well as having the excuse to move for a moment and get some hot blood flowing around an otherwise glacial corpse. Roger took his coffee and sat on a nearby bench which overlooked the River, Mersey. He sat on the far left-hand side so as to see the plaque in the middle.

> PETER DOLAN
> (02.12.1940 – 03.08.2006)
> Happy Memories on Crosby Sands
> *Never Forgotten*

Almost ten years had passed since then. The wood stain on the bench had faded considerably and the brass plaque had dulled to the lifeless brown of a battered old penny. It was a tired structure in desperate need of maintenance, but the flowers tied to the back had only just began to wilt. Clearly someone still remembered Peter Dolan enough to pay tribute to his bench. Roger always read the plaques on the benches, he viewed the act as a gesture of respect, an obligation for those who chose to sit upon them.

There was a serenity about the waves that brought a great calm over Roger. He clasped his hands together around the coffee cup and bowed his head to say a few prayers: some to God, some to absent friends. It had been a long time since Roger last said proper prayers. He found that he would always get into an argument with God when he did.

The calm was harshly interrupted by the roar of an engine tearing up the road behind the large patch of grass that separated the promenade from the nearby houses. A 2015-plate four-wheel drive had travelled down the street at an alarming speed, before braking harshly and turning into an unnecessarily large driveway. The engine was revved like hell in an effort to display its power and bring attention to the vehicle. The act chased away the nearby seagulls and starlings, before four people exited in raucous fits of laughter – the type of posh laughter that responded to terrible and long-winded jokes which ended with poor punch lines devoid of wit. *What a load of tripe.* Roger loved the beach but hated those types of people. He saw it as a crying shame that the likes of them, likely to have kicked a few people down on their way to the top, were the ones who could afford such property. He looked at them in the distance in disdain. He pondered how small, if any, a loss it would be to the world if they were to just disappear, perhaps as the result of a mass cull by the good Lord like in the book of Revelations. The idea of it made him smile to himself. Roger was more of a light believer than a Bible-thumper.

Throwing his hand and his head back to enjoy the last

swig of coffee, Roger threw his paper cup in the bin and then began to make his way back to his car. It was about a 20-minute walk to the other car park. Roger did not mind. The sound of the wind and waves, as well as the lack of visitors to the beach, made it even more tranquil. Anthony Gormley's iron men were lucky individuals as far as he was concerned.

The little trip out had temporarily exorcised Roger's mind of the worst of the demons that normally occupied it, though he was well aware of the fact that they always came back. He paused along the way, put his hands on the semi-rusted railings and looked across the Mersey at the Wirral. He thought about the recent body that had turned up at New Brighton beach. It had been the main story for just over a week on the local news, but it was soon forgotten. Just four weeks had passed and a story only stayed hot for so long in the modern day media. Only police, close friends and family of the victim were still questioning what had gone on and why the person had been chosen in what was looking more and more like the work of a serial killer. Roger had often found it amazing how people forget big events so easily in life, wondering whether it was a case of some things being too horrific to focus on for too long, or just the ignorance of post-millennium humanity – *whatever; for the case it was probably for the best.*

SIX

Thursdays were usually ironing days, but Linda was taking a break today. Mick had enough work shirts for a few days, and Linda was pretty tired after Benny had suffered a bad nightmare and was too scared to go to sleep again. One of the villains from a Disney film he had recently watched had scared him. Mick had gone off to work shouting that Linda was too soft, and that if he had an accident that day then she would be to blame.

Linda liked to think she was selfless, but she knew deep down inside that she could be anything but that sometimes. That selfish side of her had come out the previous night when she decided that it was not fair that Mick should sleep while she was stuck awake with Benny. She woke Mick and made an almighty fuss until he grudgingly stayed up too. The way she had relentlessly harped on at him, he would have had little option had he decided to try to get back to sleep.

Linda often felt like Mick was losing interest in her but put it down to the long shifts sapping his passion and drive for life away. She would often offer to go back to working for the government, but he was always authoritatively insistent that she remain at home for Benny.

"No son of mine is going to grow up thinking a babysitter is his mother!" It was a regular statement in their Benny-related arguments, especially after Mick had downed a few beers.

More than eight weeks had passed since the grisly murder in New Brighton, and Linda was still very upset that her husband thought she was overreacting. She had been threatened a few times before in work when turning people down for disability benefit and had always feared someone wanting vengeance. With the most recent victim being a job centre employee, it further fuelled the all-consuming inferno of her fear. The police made a public statement: they had decided that the recent killings were indeed linked. The only real thing these morbid occurrences had in common with each other was torture of the most horrid kind. Linda knew it was ridiculous to think that these had anything to do with her, but the fact that a spree of murders had spread to Merseyside was an alarming one indeed. Though only a short distance over the water, Linda often viewed Wirral as a different country – as though it was part of Wales – but recent events had made it very clear to her that it was merely a stone's throw away: far too close for comfort.

Despite her fears, Linda had worked hard at not letting everything get to her too much. As far as she was concerned, the less the news spoke about it, the better. It had taken two weeks before she could put Merseytalk on again without the fear of hearing details. Linda knew what had happened to the others: fingers missing, tongues yanked out – there was even one instance where someone was left hanging by their mouth – on a hook like a fish, with their hands bound behind their back to prevent escape. Hearing all this wasn't as bad when it was all miles away in cities and towns she had no connection to. Linda wanted to know nothing more of this most recent horror-movie recreation over the river.

The radio crackled slightly but the dial was as close to 106.8fm as it possibly could be. The Merseytalk jingle came on and the day's topic was the increase in miscreant youths on 'scrambler bikes.' To many other parts of the country it was a strange term; in Liverpool, battered motorbikes unfit for road use had been given a nickname by the police and were now as much a part of the local lingo as 'ciggies' and 'the bizzies,' courtesy of the countless local news headlines in which they featured. They had been terrorising countless estates throughout the city, and people were calling in to complain that the police were not doing enough to fight the issue, insisting that they were more concerned with handing out traffic fines or giving talks to school children. The presenter, as usual, sat on the fence during the discussions. At one point, he attempted to sympathise with the youths when a very angry caller had insisted they must be imprisoned or castrated. Even though she knew the presenter was just doing his job, Linda was perplexed at how he could even feign sympathy for these thugs that scared the living daylights out of hundreds of local residents. She was grateful that there was not much of this type of thing in Crosby, certainly not on Acacia Avenue where her two-hundred-and-fifty-grand house seemed to spare her such disturbances.

In this part of Liverpool, the biggest problem she had to worry about was the paperboy not delivering the Echo.

Having a house worth the same as the big prize on Deal or No Deal certainly had its benefits, and as upset as she had been when her parents both died within the same year of each other, the house they left behind changed her life. Bought for just £4000 back in the late 1950s, the detached bungalow in Formby fetched a whopping £275,000 when it was sold in 2006, just before the global recession. Linda went from a basic two-bedroom flat in Waterloo to the luxury life that she was now enjoying in almost the blink of an eye. Ugly, foul-mouthed neighbours; Staffordshire bull terriers that never stopped barking and a constant smell of damp became a thing of the past in an instant. She knew that should feel lucky but deep down, she felt more like she deserved it.

Benny was going to a friend's house for tea, and Linda predicted that Mick would likely pass out as soon as he got in due to his lack of sleep the previous night. With those two facts in mind, she deemed herself free of obligations and decided to open the wine early. She poured out her idea of a large glass, filling it to the brim: an amount that would equal at least two large measures in a pub. John Lewis sold ridiculously large glasses which were more for show than anything, but Linda considered it a crime not to make the best use of the full capacity when the occasion presented itself. Merseytalk had just about finished, and she flicked the TV on to see what was on the news.

Her hand gripped the glass tighter as she saw the yellow 'breaking news' bar at the bottom, the black letters disappearing into the left pane before reappearing in the right. There had been another killing. Just when her crimson-painted nails might have dug into and shattered the delicate drinking vessel, her grip loosened just in time. The next body had been found in Deansgate, Manchester. This one had been found bound in a wheelchair, which initial police speculation suggested was for ease of movement. As usual, they refrained from drawing any links to the other killings that had taken place. The thought that even someone 99 pence short of a pound could deduce this was the same style had slightly amused Linda as her mind began to wander.

Linda imagined the murderer as a weedy little man, with a weasel-like face and lank hair, too weak to even dispose of his victim without aid. She did not believe that it could be a woman and the media had fallen out of love with the idea of it being a cult following snippets of information which they had been drip-fed during police press conferences. Linda could imagine this time, she could think about it. She was not particularly fazed by it, even though Manchester was just a short trip up the M62: the crime was not on her metaphorical doorstep this time. The view from her and Mick's bedroom window looked out onto the River Mersey and New Brighton was easily visible on a clear day. There had been something about that which made the previous murder so unsettling. Manchester may as well have been London as far as Linda was concerned: she was just relieved it was elsewhere.

The news moved onto the next story: an old man was facing a criminal record for feeding pigeons, a sad tale but more light-hearted than the main story. Linda drew the large glass to her lips and was surprised to find it empty already: the news had made for thirsty watching. She sauntered to the kitchen with the kind of confident walk the first drink can give a girl and refilled her glass to a level far higher than it was intended for, making it look almost like one of the novelty birthday glasses found in card shops. Benny would not be getting brought back until 9pm and Mick was gone until midnight. She chuckled to herself that she might even have another few beverages before they return, emphatically informing her conscience that she deserved it.

SEVEN

Being a judge was never easy. Roger was realising that increasingly as each day dawned. He had never really wanted the job, but he had found himself doing it all the same. The latest case had been a real shocker: a negligent doctor, the kind of typical character one might find at a standard NHS surgery. He would sit there, gaze at the patient whilst not taking in the majority of what they were saying and pick up on a few key words. Then, he would either pass them on to the Accident and Emergency department at the local hospital, refer them to a specialist of some form or hand them a green slip and send them to the pharmacy: *anything* to get them out of his office as quickly as possible.

Every day there were queues, and Dr. Watson always wanted to be rid of them as quickly as possible. Queues meant late nights; late nights meant longer waits for chilled Chardonnay and a Marks and Spencer's meal for two with his trophy wife in their semi-detached Lydiate home. Dr. Watson had been denied of these comforts in the courtroom, though. He had been on trial for a very serious crime and it was made clear to him that he would not to return to such comforts unless he had been found innocent. Many had fallen victim to his negligence, but he had been on trial for his actions against one patient in particular.

A man had been worried about cancer and had done as the television adverts and posters advised: booked an appointment with his GP after having had a bad cough for over a month. That GP happened to be Dr Watson in the 5:45pm slot. The doctor had been due to finish at 6pm but queues meant that the man did not enter his room until 6:03pm and – with three more people to come after him – the doctor treated the appointment like a hundred-metre sprint.

Roger had sat and listened as the defendant pleaded his case. He could see through this middle-come-upper-class vermin, spilling his guts and blubbering like a baby as the prosecution gave a scathing onslaught of the disinterested doctor's actions – or lack of them. Three times in total the late patient had visited Dr. Watson, and only on the third time had he admitted them to hospital. By then it was far too late: the verdict was indeed cancer and it had spread. Everything came out in court. Watson cried as he begged and pleaded his case: sobbing that it was not his fault, he was having problems at home; he was having to work too long hours due to NHS budget cuts. Judge Birch listened to it all. He was a shrewd man and had no second thoughts when it came to dealing the doctor a life-changing sentence.

Roger needed a break after that last case, the scale of it all took it out of him: the way some rich bastard could cause the death of his patient and show virtually no emotion until he was actually up in the courtroom was something else. Many thought that judges lived very comfortable lives, but it was evident from the delicate balance of whiskey during the night-time, paracetamol and anti-depressants throughout the day, that Roger was no jobsworth.

Roger had decided to visit the City Centre that morning, a place him and his father enjoyed going together very much for a few beers and a few bets. He stopped off and placed a five-pound win on 'Dreamer' in the 2:05 at Newmarket in the betting shop that he used to take his dad to. It had been independently owned by the same family for decades but had recently been taken over by a large chain: they had made an offer that was too good to waste any amount of time considering sentimental value. The old owners had refused to have even a fruit machine in their shop due to the ilk of customer that they attract. Four fixed-odds betting terminals were added as soon as the big firm took over, with more than 10 different versions of roulette on each one.

Old Billy Birch had often said how sad it made him to see everything going downhill: huge superstores being erected led to derelict streets decorated with shuttered buildings, where there had once been all manner of thriving small businesses. Roger often sat and listened to his dad tell him such tales of when doors could be left unlocked, when everyone in a street knew each other's name and would socialise.

"Those were the days, son." He would say with a glint of nostalgia mixed with sadness in his eyes.

Billy was sadly now just a memory as much as those past days were. That was a fact that Roger found every day that he just could not come to terms with. Everyone who knew his father thought a lot of him: a kind, respectable and caring man that had put a lot into life. His wife Annie, had died very young as a result of throat cancer. Roger had never really got to know his mum too well, though he had a few memories of her for which he was grateful. Billy had done his best to bring his son up well and give him a good life. Roger had made sure to return the favour when his dad became less able in his old age, though he made sure that the diamond geezer retained his independence: to take that from him would have been akin to handing out a death sentence.

A pint of bitter and a few bets on the gee-gees had always made for a great afternoon though, on his most recent visit to the city centre, Roger was not able to manage more than one bet and thought better of going to the pub. The betting shop alone was too much right now, as the lump in his throat was reminding him. His bet had lost but it meant nothing: the wager was just a gesture, though the fact that his horse was called 'Dreamer' felt symbolic. *Dashed dreams more like.* Staving off the temptation of booze in this instant – he tried to when he could – Roger instead went and sat upstairs in a coffee shop on the edge of Liverpool One shopping complex. He parked himself right by the large window which looked out onto Church Street: it was filled with people. The new shopping complex was big and flashy, but Roger liked the fact that Church Street still outshone L1, as it was nicknamed, on most occasions. A coffee and a peaceful environment helped clear his mind. A few silent tears had fallen as his mind wandered, but Roger knew the dam had to spring a leak or two every now and again.

EIGHT

It had been a considerable amount of time since the UK had endured the company of a serial killer. The police had not wanted to concede that the ongoing countrywide murders were linked, but the media had stoked the fire so much that the PR department of Scotland Yard had to cut its losses and give in to the looming wave of scrutiny, stating that they now believed the killings to be linked but only by the manner in which the victims were made to suffer.

The national newsreader stood in front of a North Wales police station and announced that another person had been killed in the Welsh seaside town of Rhyl. The body of a youth had been dumped down a side street. The murder had not taken place in that location – the all too familiar grizzly torture routine had taken place first somewhere else. The body had been identified as that of Joseph Conlon, 19, originally from the Bootle area. His DNA records provided police with his identity: they had his information on file. His short life had been marred with a string of arrests, and he had finally faced jail time for an arson attack the previous year.

The body was unrecognisable: his hands and feet had peen pulped, most likely with a hammer or some form of blunt instrument. A once gaunt and unpleasant face was now incomparable to the photo on the prisoner dis-

31

charge card. All teeth had been removed: some with blunt force, others with tools; a few fragments still lay embedded in the gums. The end of the nose had been sliced off with a knife – a blunt one, judging by the jagged cutting method – and the worst part was how the eyes had been gouged out and left to hang on their stalks of ropey tissue which bound them to the body. It looked like something out of a Hammer horror film: one of the scenes that look too ridiculous to be real, except this was indeed real. It had been no quick death. The boy had suffered immensely prior to his untimely departure from the world.

The victim had been living in a bail house since his release from HMP Walton. The tag on his leg would have led police right to where the torture took place had it been one of the latest versions. Unfortunately for police, the tag was one of the older models and was only able to set off an alarm should curfew be broken. It could not provide any GPS history. Despite the feet being bloody, blob-like stumps, the killer had made sure not to break the tag, knowing it could lead police to their exact location if its alarm was triggered.

The news report focused more on the latest police statement and what actions were being taken to catch this killer, or killers, than the death of a miscreant youth. He had not been a model character in his life and it was revealed that he had received several anti-social be-haviour orders prior to his eventual incarceration for crimes such as robberies, gross bodily harm and domes-tic violence. A sound bite played the voice of his parole officer, it sounded somewhat muffled as though it had been recorded from a phone call.

"This lad had many enemies but surely none who would go to these lengths to end his life."

With such a dark introduction to the news yet again, when the story concluded the reporter sounded relieved as he took the opportunity to highlight the upcoming feature: a dancing rescue cat that had captured the hearts of the nation. Linda listened to the end of the news as she lit a cigarette and carried on preparing her salad. It was nice to have a light story at the end, and even though the killer had struck again, the information on the victims' crimes left her unsympathetic towards the manner of his death. She even felt slightly glad that the killer had found him: *one less waste of space to worry about in the world.*

Linda had quit smoking when she had got pregnant with Benny but had sparked up her old habit again following continued rows with Mick. She had been upping the amount of wine she was drinking and grown tired of her husband coming in and expecting a meal to be prepared. Linda was forever dieting and abhorred needing to prepare big, carbohydrate-laden meals at all hours for her husband when he was more than capable of doing them himself. She always had a bowl of salad in the fridge and didn't see why he could not make do with that. Mick worked hard and liked a decent meal after a long day, but after coming home one night to a note highlighting the greens in the fridge, he made the mistake of questioning his wife's level of wine consumption as the possible reason for his lack of stodgy food: an error which caused a huge argument and saw the demise of several plates and a jar of instant coffee.

The couple were at loggerheads. Mick was still being the same man he had always been, but Linda had seemingly grown tired of her husband in recent weeks. They had never been ultra close, but hostilities were generally few and far between. A constant bad atmosphere shrouded the house, and they both knew a divorce was looming. The marriage only came about in the first place because Linda got pregnant, and that only occurred because she had been forgetting to take her contraceptive pills as often as she should.

During an argument the previous week, Mick had even blurted out that he only proposed because Linda got pregnant. She had always known it, but hearing him actually say it had only made her despise him even more. The expensive Crosby home that looked pleasant and quaint on the outside was anything but that on the inside. Mick hated smoke and Linda rekindling her relationship with her pungent friends was just another way of punishing him: she wanted to anger him. She was just about sick of him and the life she was leading. The big house was nice, but she missed the fearsome, results-driven go-getter that she used to be. As a housewife she never felt truly respected. She was not sure if it was due to the extra wine she had been enjoying lately, but she had found herself having come to hate her husband; Linda wanted to live her life *her* way. *If he stood in that path then he deserved everything he got.*

Noon was approaching, and Mick had been on night shifts this past March. His car pulled up the driveway early today, and he plodded in, his face red and eyes heavy. He made a noise as if to say "alright" but it was forced and incoherent: the greeting a person will give to a colleague that they do not care for.

"Why are you back now?" She enquired in a teacher-esque tone, "I thought you were in until 12?"

"What does it look like? Do I look like a well man to you?" Retorted Mick, after a snort of inward breath through blocked nostrils.

"Don't you talk to me like that: I won't put up with your bad attitudes with me anymore. Apologise, now!"

Mick gave his nose a hearty blow with a wad of kitchen roll. She *hated* him using the kitchen roll to blow his nose: she always insisted he use toilet paper. "You're the one with the attitude: day-in-day-out digs. I work hard – hard enough for you to be able to be a housewife – and these days, all you do is get pissed, and now you can't even be bothered cooking."

"You deserve it, the way you carry on. It's not hard what you do. Why should I cook for you? I eat healthily. If you don't, then that's your problem – and stop using the kitchen roll to blow your nose: it's disgusting!" Mick had grabbed a cup and was in the process of making himself a cup of tea, another pleasantry Linda had abandoned, but upon hearing her most recent comment he launched the cup at the wall and clenched his jaw. Bosses, and people he hated spoke to him like that, but he was not about to put up with it from the woman who shared his surname; they may have been at odds but he would not accept being spoken down to. A thousand thoughts went through Mick's head. He was scared of being a part-time dad whose contact would be restricted to weekend McDonald's meetings with his son, but this had to stop. Linda had been acting like a child with silent contempt for weeks on end now, going out of her way to make him feel small on the occasions when she did actually speak and making it clear that she held no affection for him.

As far as Mick was concerned, whatever they may once have had was long gone. His mind scanned through all the reservations he had about what problems leaving Linda may bring, but he was too young to resign his life to the harpy that his wife had turned into and certainly could not manage another 10 years of it until Benny finished school, grew up and left home.

The cup smashing had shocked Linda, and Mick have her a repulsed glance as he stormed upstairs and filled his duffel bag, usually reserved for holidays, with a heap of clothes, shoes and anything else which meant he would not need to return to the house for a very long time. He had made up his mind. Some decisions are best mulled over, but Mick was finished with it all. As he descended back down the stairs, he saw his wife standing in front of the door with her arms folded: even then, condescending – like a headmistress glaring at a naughty pupil.

"Where do you think you're going?" She asked in an inquisitive yet menacing tone.

"As far away from you as I can *possibly* get. You speak of disgusting before? I'll tell you what's disgusting, you!"

Linda slapped her husband as he said this, hard. He had not been able to block it because he had hold of the duffel bag with both hands due to the weight of it with everything he had thrown in. He dropped it and put a hand to his face and felt blood, a result of the nails that no doubt his money had gone towards getting manicured at the salon. She went to slap him again, but he seized her right arm this time.

"Get off, you're hurting me!" She shouted as she tried to hit him with her left arm. Mick seized this too, and she started kicking out at him, aiming for where it would hurt most. Mick dodged as he fought to calm his writhing wife, but then a tremendous pain shot through him as she sank her teeth into the top of his hand above his knuckles, where the thin section of skin between his index finger and thumb tore open easily and a sticky red liquid oozed out. The pain caused him to throw her to the floor, more from reaction than intention.

Linda looked up at her husband in outright hatred: the fall had hurt her. She realised that there would be no going back from this and, even though she despised him at that moment, the idea of him leaving filled her with malevolent hatred: she was far too good to be walked out on by him. Without any concern for his downed wife, Mick walked to the kitchen roll and attempted to tear off a lengthy amount to place upon his bleeding hand. The pain of his injury limited his dexterity and so he picked up the entire roll with the intention of addressing the wound once he was out of the house – he just wanted to get away from *her* and the situation he was in at that moment.

He made his way back to the front door and picked his bag up, this time with one hand – the stress of the situation summoned a greater strength from within. In his other hand, he clutched the kitchen roll; the act of gripping it made blood ooze through the layers of tissue. Linda, who had remained lying on the floor in shock, knew this would be the final curtain for their marriage and rose up before charging at her husband with a manic scream. He saw the punch coming and caught it, shoving her into the wall. This time it *was* intentional. Linda hit the deck and Mick swung the front door open and walked out into the front garden towards his car for what he knew would be the final time.

"Bastard. You'll never see your son again!"

She screamed after him from the doorway as he threw his duffel bag into the boot of his Peugeot 306, parked on the driveway. It was an old vehicle, but it was reliable. Mick was just about to get into the car when he looked at the bloodied kitchen roll in his hand, complete with holder. He turned around to face Linda and shoved the whole roll up to his nose, which was streaming due to both his cold and the burning pain in his hand, and blew as hard as he could in a derisory gesture. After this he threw it into the air and kicked it in the direction of the house before holding a middle finger up to his wife. In his mind he knew it was somewhat of a childish gesture, but he felt mighty good for having done it. Had Benny been home, he would have controlled himself more, but the fact that his lad was at school and had not had to witness the events that took place was a blessing to Mick. He sped away with his 1.6-litre engine drowning out most of the insults and obscenities that she had run to the end of the driveway to scream at him upon her realisation that he was actually leaving her.

Mick stopped the car for a few seconds and took one brief glance in his rear view mirror to see the monster he was leaving behind. The facial expressions she was pulling were almost demonic, and he could not believe that he had spent all those years with her without realising just what venom she had in her. As bad as matters seemed at that moment, Mick was glad it had happened. He found himself frightened at the idea that he could have carried on in the marriage, never truly knowing the evil his wife held inside her. He drove away with no idea of where he would go to or what he would do: the faecal matter had only just begun to hit the fan, and he knew that she would use Benny against him. Roundabouts, road signs and traffic lights passed through his field of vision as his mind struggled to make sense of the day and formulate a plan of action. Despite his current mental turmoil, one feeling overrode everything else in Mick's head: *relief*.

NINE

Roger usually had patience for youths, especially remorseful ones, but in this day and age, they all seemed to be getting increasingly nasty. Hate-filled scum that were going to be the next generation: the end of the world would be more beneficial to humanity – *indeed it would.*

The day's defendant was charged with a heap of offences: a list a mile long. He'd had chance after chance, but continued to mock the justice system. That was until he came face to face with the honourable Judge Birch. The boy's latest crime was one too far, one he had thought that he had 'gotten away with' after police found little to no evidence that would help the prosecution.

The boy showed no remorse as he was reminded of his vile actions against one old man. It had been a dare from friends to throw stones at the old man's car, who had emerged from his house and tried to chase the boy. The little bastard had known all too well that there was nothing to fear. Police cuts meant a far lower street presence of bobbies on the beat and the old man could not touch him, or he would press charges: assaulting a youth was far worse than throwing a few stones as far as police were concerned. The boy had mocked the old man who confronted him, backing away whilst teasing him. He had not expected the old-timer to be able to grab hold of his collar and pin him to the bonnet of the car.

Sadly, the old man did not have the strength he used to and was caught afoul of a back headbutt. That was bad enough but the youth, angered that his friends had laughed at his initial error, decided to flaunt his skills in order to recover any street face that may have been lost. He kicked the old man in the shin. A withered leg quickly gave way as the man cried out upon hitting the cold, hard concrete floor. He had been a strong man once, mentally *and* physically. He had lost his wife many moons ago but made the best of raising a happy family. Now the old man lay in agony, looking up at the shaven-headed, beady-eyed, spotty youth who had likely broken his leg or, at the very least, fractured it. The boy grinned as he booted the car, putting a big dent in the passenger-side door. He was wearing an oversized sovereign ring and punched the passenger window. The fool thought it would break easier and his audience of friends cackled with laughter as he flailed his hand around in pain after only managing to crack it. In an effort to once again look tough, the boy raised his leg high and kicked the wing mirror off in one go. The old man grabbed his leg and a weakened voice tried to reason with the miscreant youth amidst laboured breaths.

"Please... stop. I need... I need that car. Just go I won't... call... the police."

"Get the f★★★ off me, you stupid old c★★★!"

The boy practically spat out his retort as he kicked the old man in the ribs – and again in the hip – as his sadistic friends cheered and cackled away like a bunch of hyenas. The man let out an excruciating-yet-breathless cry as blood ran from his mouth. Only then had the boy panicked and decided to disappear, unrepentant for his actions and only ceasing them because he feared the sentence he may receive if he had killed the old guy.

There were no witnesses but the crowd who watched. The old man did not die: he made it back into his house and convinced his family that he had suffered a fall. He did not call the police, it was embarrassing to have ended up so frail, and he only envisaged more problems if he pursued the issue. He had thought that nobody would want to listen to an old man anyway.

Roger had unearthed a full confession from the defendant with a little unorthodox persuasion. He followed his own rules and guidelines. He was never one for tales of the devil or demons, but he truly believed that – right there and then – something from hell stood before him: a heartless creature fuelled by venom and hatred. He saw filth like this as sub-human and beyond redemption – and he did not believe it was possible to fix something that was so broken to begin with. The boy still stood remorseless, convinced that he was untouchable, not realising that he was soon to learn otherwise.

TEN

Linda was enjoying having the house to herself. With Mick gone she had so much more time to do what she wanted without being scrutinised or needing to cook as often. An envelope full of money was put through the letterbox once a week which enabled Mick to take his boy to the park. It was an unspoken agreement but Mick knew that he had to do this, or his wife would make his life hell. He had been living in the spare room of his friends' flat and looked pretty rough as he arrived at the house, walking up the flagged path – which he had laid it himself, along the grass, soon after they had bought the property. He rang the doorbell – which he had fitted with utmost precision so as to ensure neatness and that no draught got through. There was no answer. He pressed the button again and the bell sounded once more, the three-chime electric sound reverberating loud enough to be heard throughout the house. Inside, Linda knew he was there but took her time anyway just to be awkward.

At first, she hadn't wanted her husband to go: she did not want to be walked out on – Linda had always done the dumping in her life, not the other way around. She smirked to herself as she heard the letterbox get pushed up and heard Mick call her name. She could see the door from the top of the stairs, but he could not see her.

A loud succession of foul language was uttered as Mick began to walk back to his car. Just as he reached the gate, Linda opened the door. Mick knew this would be the case: it was the same crap every week with some minor alteration for creativity; he only put up with it for the sake of seeing Benny. This week he was in for another unpleasant surprise.

"He's not well today." The words forced out of Linda's lips as brief, emotionless and cold as possible.

"What's wrong with him?"

"Fever. He needs rest. Not allowed out."

Mick gritted his teeth. He knew it was rubbish: he had known the woman well enough to know that her more common tongue was more audible when she was lying. That way of using as few words as possible always sounded rough, just like she was before they met – long before the put-on posh voice was adopted. "You could've let me know."

Linda just stared blankly. She thought that she was quite funny and it made Mick lose what little resolve he had maintained. He turned back to his car and shouted loud enough for the entire avenue to hear.

"Argh, suit yourself then you vindictive sow!" Mick almost took the gate off its hinges as he slammed it and left the property before revving his car as loud as possible and bombing off down the usually tranquil, tree-lined avenue.

Linda waited until she knew he was out of sight and then gave a smug grin to herself. Benny loved his dad, but as far as she was concerned, Mick didn't deserve to see him. Children were easily bribed and Benny had been given something impossible to refuse to an 8-year-old boy: the latest FIFA video-game. Usually Linda was ultra strict when it came to allowing her son gaming time on his Xbox 360. She tried to make him wait and save up his pocket money to buy things he wanted: she had intended to teach him patience and money management, but in this instance she was happy to put her own interests first. Benny normally bolted down the stairs when his dad came over, but he had been holed-up in his bedroom with the volume extra loud on his television and his face four inches away from the screen on his new game. He had hardly noticed that the bell had rung.

As Benny won another match, the culmination of his morning and afternoon efforts making him 12 points clear at the top of the league table, Linda told her son to come down for his tea. Whilst sat at the table, Benny asked:

"Mum, why hasn't dad came today?"

"I don't know son, he hasn't been in touch at all."

"But dad *always* comes to see me on a Sunday, I wanted to show him my new game."

"I don't know what he's been doing today, he's got his new life that he's been leading. He's probably busy. Maybe I can come and see – you can show him next week if he comes?"

Benny gave a smile that was more to please his mum than express his feelings: the boy was feeling abandoned for the first time in his life. Linda smiled and gave her son a hug from behind and a kiss on the cheek.

"I'll always be here for you, son. I'll never let you down."

ELEVEN

William Archibald Birch was a man of what are regarded in the modern day as 'old school' values. A true gentleman, he was polite and courteous without being condescending or patronising. He was a hard worker and had served as a joiner for the majority of his life. Everyone knew Billy; everyone respected Billy: even the rough kids who did not care who they offended. Billy never spent much on himself: a few pints of bitter and a few winners on the horses were perfect for him – though the winners were not as easily sought out as the pints of Cains. Billy bought Cains because he liked to support local businesses and saw no reason for companies to ship things across the country when they could just as easily be made closer to home. Even his usual dress of black shoes, jeans, a short-sleeved shirt and a beige jacket were all purchased from the different stores of Liverpool City Centre. He loved the city.

Billy had struggled after losing his wife to cancer shortly after their son was born. He had pressed on in life and was excellent at his trade: he never went short of work. As his age increased, his jet black hair turned slowly to salt-and-pepper and then to grey, and he started to lose the strength of youth he had enjoyed. Many of his friends had died, almost all were smokers, but Billy had stopped the day his wife was diagnosed with throat cancer. She had never smoked herself, but he often felt a twinge of guilt that he may have caused the untimely demise of his beloved, Mary, by having smoked in her presence quite a lot.

Billy had taken on a young apprentice to help him in his trade, as the physical graft was taking a lot out of him. He had liked the idea of passing on his tried and tested skills on to a new recruit of the trade, but he soon realised that he was just delaying the inevitable. At 62, he was too young and too poor to retire. He had three years to go before he could claim his state pension. Billy did not have a private pension: he had worked for himself most of his life and always had just about enough to get by on.

With great reluctance he had applied for Disability Living Allowance, DLA, which he had hoped would see him through until he could draw his state pension and hang up his boots for good. Being the man he was, he wanted to work whilst he was able. He never wanted to be seen as a scrounger, but his chest was awful, and he had begun feeling tired a lot of the time. Even simple tasks were beginning to take a lot of effort. He had worked hard all of his life but initially refused to claim any benefit, let alone disability, as a matter of pride.

His son, Roger, had eventually convinced him to feel justified in trying to obtain some help after convincing his dad to share his views on the amount of work-shy young people in existence, as well as foreigners that were coming into the country and being given considerable financial aid despite having put nothing into the system.

It was a record which mainstream media played most days and one which those who felt hard-done-by in life found catchy and easy to listen to. A long and drawn-out application was made for the DLA benefit. Billy had filled in countless forms, providing a clear argument that he was not fit for work. He attended a medical assessment, being run by an American company that the government paid to perform tests on those seeking disability benefit. He was initially turned down after being asked to perform an abundance of tasks that were not in any way related to why he was claiming. His ability to make a circle with his thumb and index finger or raise his hands above his head were not the causes of him being unable to work. He appealed the initial decision as was his legal right and was invited to a more in depth interview with a senior assessor.

His second assessment saw him sat opposite a mousy woman with a hard face, who he could tell was one cold 'bitch' the moment that he had the misfortune to have walked into her office. She was wearing a suit with very high heels, and her brunette hair was yanked back off her head, revealing a set of small, almost round, ears which stuck out from the sides of her head like small satellites. Billy never claimed to be a genius, but he was a shrewd man and generally summed people up well. From the moment he laid eyes on this woman, he had a bad feeling: his initial suspicions proved to be correct as she showed no emotion throughout his one-hour appeal.

He had explained how bad he felt in his overall health in general and spent the entire time feeling belittled and ridiculed as he completed more bizarre tests, none of which related in any way as to his reason for claiming. Even the tone of voice in which he was spoken to was similar to how an adult addresses a child. At the end of it all he was told he would receive a letter detailing the outcome of the decision made. Billy knew that he did not need to wait for a brown envelope delivered by Royal Mail, second-class, to find out what that would be. Roger had sat at the back of the office and kept his mouth shut for almost the entire assessment so as not to ruin his dad's chances. He had asked a few select questions and maintained a stare at the woman – which grew into a glower as the questions got more bizarre and testing. Billy was left feeling both upset and embarrassed. His son had remained like a shadow so as to give him maximum independence and dignity, but the entire assessment left him devoid of both. It was not easy getting old but some of the bad cards life dealt Billy certainly did not make it any easier. He sang a line from an old Rolling Stones song to his son on the way down the stairs of the building.

"Oh it's such a drag getting old."

Being thrust into the world of work again at 62 years of age was a living nightmare for Billy. He knew only joinery: it had been his career, and he had never deviated from it in all his years. He was a grafter, but being unable to carry out many of the jobs he was best at left him with few decent options in his job search. As a man who'd grown up in an entirely different era, he struggled greatly as he tried to navigate a new world of CVs, group interviews and health and safety. His son, Roger, helped him apply for a number of jobs in builders merchants – but nobody wanted to employ an old man who was likely to need time off sick and would probably not be worth the money spent on training. Roger was left deeply frustrated. He knew just how great a worker his dad was, but sadly the world of employment did not see anyone over the age of 50 as sought-after, regardless of their credentials.

After attending a tedious amount of 'back to work' interviews and 'group workshops' organised by the job centre, Billy eventually landed himself a position at a large supermarket. It was a part-time, 16-hour contract but required him to work full-time hours filling shelves. Securing the role had been incredibly drawn out as Billy had been forced to endure three stages of interviews, in-cluding a voluntary afternoon of bag packing and build-ing a house out of raw spaghetti and marshmallows. Billy had thought the latter was some sort of practical joke at first, but he was glad that he had kept his thoughts to himself: he later realised it was considered a task most serious by the people in suits who had organised the re-cruitment process.

Initially, the store had seemed like a nice enough place to work – a refuge for older people who were in the familiar position of struggling to find work but were too old to pursue a new career. All of that all changed very quickly for Billy. A Hitler-esque supervisor loved making his life a misery, constantly harrying him along whilst questioning his abilities when he struggled – particularly with the handheld scanner and price gun, which was made even more difficult to use thanks to a screen lacking in calibration and the lack of a stylus.

Billy was one of the few people in the store who could add up the prices as well as any electronic till system – in fact he was often faster as more than 10 items in a transaction usually resulted in the till slowing down and stuttering. His skills did not matter though, despite seeming a friendly and welcoming work environment, it was clear that he had been taken on to satisfy an equal opportunities figure in a report somewhere: something the store could highlight to government officials with a smug grin at how they do not exclude the elderly. This was not the case at all: they took them on, but they did not treat them as well as the younger, up-and-coming staff members. Billy learned every day that a man of his age was not at all what the company really wanted. Young men in tight suits with winkle-picker shoes were all the rage. But even if he still had his youth, he would never be caught dead in that attire.

Within weeks of working for the company, the lack of a pulse was becoming increasingly enticing as Billy's mind began to question the point in trying anymore. There were a few other people close to his age in the store. Nobody dared speak up to the bosses: their roles there would likely be their last ones before their retirement, and they were desperate to see them out – enduring whatever often-humiliating treatment they were dealt. Billy had been desperate to maintain his independence, but the job was making him a nervous wreck. He knew of people who went to the doctor to get signed off sick with nerves, but he was too proud to even consider anything like that: he did not want to be seen as some kind of gibbering wreck.

Billy continued to press on until one unbearable day when the supervisor hounded him relentlessly. There was a promotion taking place which involved offering every customer a discounted bar of chocolate. Billy was doing just that, but he was deemed not to be trying hard enough to sell them. He had never enjoyed sales, and believed that if people said no then they did not want to make an additional purchase. It was not even that good of a deal anyway – just a menial discount of 20p on an already inflated price. The supervisor knew this, but insisted that Billy carry out three different persuasion attempts with every customer. The whole thing made him very uncomfortable and several customers gave an emphatic 'no' on the third attempt – so he stopped asking and continued doing his normal job. The sadistic supervisor had been stood within ample hearing distance as several customers had their transactions processed with only one offer of the cut-price chocolate bar being made. He had taken great pleasure in striding over to old Billy Birch and singling him out in front of his fellow colleagues. A tirade of questions were barked in a tone most demeaning. As the supervisor moved uncomfortably close towards him in a menacing manner, Billy could taste the nauseating stench of stale cigarettes on his breath.

"Do you not understand what I asked you to do? Do

you realise there are people out there who'd give their right arm for this job opportunity? Just because you're polite and friendly with customers doesn't mean I can't see through you. Do you think you're some sort of rebel?"

Billy had retained his resolve throughout the humiliating ordeal – but enough was enough. With both hands, he shoved the supervisor with such force that he almost fell backwards. He spoke emphatically through gritted teeth as he powered towards the supervisor, getting right in his face as the lanky little Hitler had done to him just seconds before.

"And just who do you think you are, mate? Big man, are you? Picking on everyone in here? No bugger likes you – is it any wonder? You'd best lay off pal: I've had enough of it. I've had it up to here with you!" Billy may have been old on the outside, but he was still in his twenties in his mind, and he certainly felt it again with that shove. Billy glared at him right in the eyes. The supervisor was grimacing back at him, and a silence had befallen the entire till area whilst staff and customers alike had become spectators.

"Touch me again and I'll call the police! You're sacked: get out of my shop. I'll not tolerate this conduct! Get out right now, you old fool!" The supervisor failed to see the irony that so many onlookers saw: it was far from *his* shop, and he was not even anywhere near store manager – just someone who had kissed arse and browned his nose for so many years that he thought he was untouchable. Billy made him feel anything but untouchable, though, as he seized him by the throat and pinned him against the till counter.

"Just who the bloody hell are you to tell me how it is? Talking to me like crap, you're nothing but a little weasel!"

The supervisor yelled out as Billy's vice-like grip dug into his neck. He scratched and fought against the elderly man he had spoken down to just moments before, even his attempts at fighting back were pathetic. There he was, bested by an old man: steely blue eyes and gritted teeth looking down on him like he was nothing; at that moment that was indeed the case. Everyone else in the store feared him due to his almost intimate relationship with the company's hierarchy, the type that could only be born from extreme and extended sycophancy.

Time seemed to have gone into slow motion as he pinned a skinny, pencil-like neck against the counter. Billy looked around. He had amassed quite the audience: some looking shocked, some enjoying the show. He clocked one old woman scurrying to the store pay-phone. Her attempt to look inconspicuous would have been comical to Billy were it not for the situation. It did not take a master lip-reader to make out 'police.' There was always one do-gooder: sod's law. He let go of the struggling rodent who fell to his knees, gasping. Billy took a good look around at everyone – all the onlookers. There were a few cheers and shouts. He felt very light-headed, almost separate from his body. One of the cashiers called across to him.

"Are you alright Billy, love?"

"Yeah. Yeah, I'm okay ta. I think I'll be off home now."

It was raining outside and cold. Billy was grateful of the bad weather though: he felt red-hot inside, raging. The blood had not surged through his body like that for many a year. He was not even the aggressive type, but it had all been too much that day: the straw had well and truly broken the camel's back. His legs felt weak during the walk – almost hollow – but he managed to make it home. Straight away, he poured himself a large glass of Scotch – neat. It proved a challenging task with his visibly shaking hands – he was a nervous wreck. Billy took an initial big gulp of it and almost collapsed into his armchair. Another large gulp drained about two-thirds of the glass and Billy closed his eyes, grateful of the serenity, safe within the peace of his abode. Time passed in the form of a most abhorrent dream involving loved ones, past and present, before Billy was awakened by the electronic peal of his doorbell. A tired and lifeless voice was heard through the door.

"Merseyside Police."

Billy put as much force as he could into his arms in an effort to rise from the chair – he had felt the strongest he had been in years just hours before, and now he felt the weakest he ever had in his entire life. He opened the door and was questioned as to who he was by two police officers in their high-visibility jackets that were now standard uniform. He confirmed his name with a stammer. Deep down he knew why they were there, but at that moment, he was not capable of focusing on anything at all: even his vision was a blur. One officer was female, with a hard face like a bulldog chewing a wasp. The other was a squat young male with beady eyes, dark and close together, and a prominent double chin which was further accentuated by his helmet strap. It was the male who informed Billy that he was under arrest on suspicion of assault and began to inform him of his rights with the standard speech that Billy had only previously heard on television dramas.

The officer only got about halfway when Billy's legs buckled. He fell to the floor, hitting his head on the corner of the radiator on the way down. Blood flowed upon the carpet, the fibres seeming to greedily gulp it up as it spread across them. Billy had been as strong as the tree that was his namesake; now the deforestation of life had well and truly taken its toll, and old Mr. Birch was wilting and withering very badly.

TWELVE

Roger was sat on a bench at Crosby beach again. It was a wet and blustery spring morning, and the abject lack of visitors highlighted that it was not a popular area in the bad weather, despite beautiful views. Only gulls, the occasional Lycra-clad cyclist and one or two determined dog walkers braved the elements on this day. The coffee van was not there – it was hit and miss with the mobile hospitality unit as it never seemed to maintain any sort of regularity. Roger was not sure if the day's absence was due to weather or the fact that he was there early – either way, he had already covered the issue by throwing a thermos flask in the car with him. He used to take one out with his dad when they went places. Traditional British cafes had become difficult to find and his dad was not a fan of fancy coffee bars, so a chance to sit down somewhere nice and enjoy a little cup of not-quite-so-hot coffee never went amiss. Roger sipped and gazed at the waves, as droplets of rain gathered upon his face. The day was another tough one. He missed his dad so much, and no matter how much time went by, he could never really get to grips with the reality of it: of how it all happened, how a number of factors knitted together into one tragic tapestry which ensured the demise of Billy Birch.

Roger's jaw stiffened as he gritted his teeth: a gesture which both alleviated anger and prevented him from crying. He had a heap of guilt. He knew he would have to answer for so much when he met his maker, but such was the curse of being a judge. Decisions *had* to be made and action *had* to be taken. There was no sign of the sun today and the intensity of the rain was increasing at a dramatic rate, shifting from drizzle to a shower in the blink of an eye. Roger just stared out at the clouds above the sea in a trance, a man completely marooned upon a small island surrounded by the tempest that was his thoughts. A dog appeared suddenly, knocking Roger out of the mental state he had entered. It was a Yorkshire terrier, absolutely drenched but full of life, panting and wagging its tail. For a moment it was like everything was okay. Roger smiled, reached down and ruffled the dogs head.

"Hello there, mate!" He loved animals but with the job he did and the hours he worked he was not able to keep a dog – not even a cat.

"Watch him – he can be funny." The owner, who had caught up with his four-legged companion, gave a warning but Roger paid it no mind. *Lay off eh, mate.* He just carried on grinning and fussing the dog which was thoroughly enjoying the attention. He was most grateful to the dog for bringing him out of a dark place on this occasion; such salvation rarely came his way when struggling for purchase within the black depths of grief and despair of his mind.

Another case was looming large. He was not looking forward to it, but it needed to be dealt with and only he could do so. In his mind he was the only one capable of passing judgement on this foul individual. Fraudsters had always existed but in the modern day they preyed so much on the elderly, like a wolf lurking circling an aging and frail ewe. An old man had received a letter informing him that charges had been made on his bank account and that he needed to call to clarify that he had made such purchases. Of course the purchases never occurred and the number was fake but the many of the previous generations came from the age of innocence and trust, where handshakes were as good as signatures and a man's word was stronger than any contract. That was all long gone and the age of suspicion had sprouted in its absence and was thriving but sadly many of those who fought to give Britain the freedom it enjoyed were now victims of those whom they had saved from the tyranny of a fascist world led by a megalomaniac.

Roger was due to pass the sentence on an individual who he found particularly repulsive. A man who had organised the fraud of countless pensioners and felt no guilt about his actions whatsoever. He had walked free from court on a technicality but now he was to face Judge Birch as a new case had been opened thanks to some fresh evidence coming to light.

The defendant had been difficult to track down and appeared chained and shackled before the court. Ahmed Abdullah had remained defiant, even in that state. He looked Roger straight in the eyes as the crimes he had been found guilty of were read out to him. He grinned back at the judge – a sly and slimy smile if ever there was one. That smile faded in an instant, as the judge stiffened his sinews and bared his teeth before raising his gavel high and bringing it down with an almighty blow as he shouted out the sentence. Again and again Roger shouted, bringing the gavel down repeatedly. The defendant, once so arrogant, was rendered the complete opposite, as Judge Birch brought Ahmed Abdullah to justice.

Roger had lost it a little in the court room that day. He was on the verge of retiring and had overseen more cases than he had ever intended to when starting out. This fraudster one was a stark enough reminder of what evil nested in the darkest corners of the world, a plague upon society that needed eradicating. *Almost there; almost there.* Roger envisaged his retirement: walking through green fields, blue skies above. Peace at last, *but not yet.*

THIRTEEN

A glass of wine had no sooner been poured than it had been emptied and refilled. Linda was not at all happy and needed a pick-me-up after Mick's latest visit. He had gone out of his way to knock extra loud, to ensure Benny heard him and came running to the door before Linda could do anything about it. Mick was sick of not seeing his son. Excuse after excuse from his wife – his patience was drastically worn down with it all. Ideally, he would have liked to pursue a divorce and gain custody of his boy, but one was expensive, and the other was extremely unlikely. It was easier for him to just plod on as was – though the situation was made unnecessarily tedious by his wife.

It was a Saturday, and Mick had taken Benny to the Merseyside derby: their favourite game to go to. Linda did not enjoy the football, but if asked would say that she sat on the red side of the fence. Mick sat on the blue half and had made sure that his son did the same – he had planned to do so from the moment he found out Linda was pregnant. Despite being a game that essentially made the city come to a standstill for 90 minutes, Linda paid it no mind and had spent the afternoon simmering that she had let her guard down and allowed Mick to take her boy away. She always viewed Benny as hers: he had grown inside her for nine months; all Mick had done was help put him there, as far as she was concerned. She sat jostling the remote angrily at the TV, trying to find something to watch whilst flicking through the channels.

When times had been better, she had watched the televised matches that her husband and son attended in the hope of seeing them in the crowd. The last thing she wanted to see there and then was Mick with a smile on his face. The batteries were low in the remote, and it did not work well. Linda became increasingly frustrated as she had to jab the buttons to navigate the channels. A nature programme with the seemingly immortal voice of Bill Oddy, Clash of the Titans, Come Dine with Me. Linda whizzed through them all and eventually left it on the news as her lust for a cigarette and a large, dry white wine became insatiable. She had not wanted Mick to know of her new-found habits, but a small indulgence would likely go unnoticed.

The main story on the news was that a known fraudster, who had infamously ripped off hundreds of pensioners and got away on a technicality, had found himself the victim the so-called Neo Ripper. The press had been unable to cope without having a pet name for something so huge and current, and had provided them with this moniker. Everything required nicknames and hashtags in modern media. Some newspapers referred to the Ripper as 'it' whilst others had already decided the serial killer was a male due to their views that the damage inflicted on victims was thought only possible via the strength of a man. The grossly mutilated body of Ahmed Abdullah had been found shoved down a manhole in a run-down council estate on the edge of Birmingham. The body had been there over a week and had only been found as the smell of putrefying flesh had grown so strong that nearby children had not been able to resist the urge to pull up the immensely heavy manhole cover to see the horrors that lay beneath it.

The newsreader went on to discuss the highlights and hallmarks of this killing and how they compared with the Neo Ripper's previous killings. Some alleged experts were featured, claiming that it could be the work of a copycat killer due to the distance between where the bodies of the victims turned up. Others were saying that it was a clear link to the other killings and that the key to finding the culprit would be apparent in some way now. The police were intending to make a statement later in the day. It was at that moment Linda turned the TV off: it was boring her. In November, just a few months earlier, she had been terrified that the killings had crept all the way up to her doorstep, but in April, the brutal murder of a fraudster in Birmingham meant nothing to her. Upon that thought she recalled an old man once calling her a fraudster as he returned to her office to confront her having been denied his benefit due to her decision. He had been swiftly removed by security. At the time, the event had really upset her, but she was a different person back then. Indeed, she was a different person even just a few weeks ago. Without her husband on the scene, and with the help of her vino and nicotine, Linda was enjoying her life more than she ever thought she could do. She was care-free. She did not have to work due to the money Mick passed through. And – best of all – she had no miserable husband to look after. Sometimes she felt a twinge of guilt at how she treated her spouse: there were much worse people out there, after all. That feeling would always quickly die away, as she would recall how he spoke to her on their final day together at Acacia Avenue.

Linda had been thinking about Mick that afternoon: at first she even worried that she missed him a little, but her mixed emotions soon settled upon hatred towards the father of her child. She decided to do something for herself, something he would never have approved of. She opened her laptop and deposited some money into the account of her new found love: online bingo. Mick gave more than enough money to keep her quiet and happy – she knew that he would do anything to see his son, and he knew that Linda was easily appeased with money. She always made sure that Benny was well looked after, but if there was a little left over, and she got to indulge in a few little pleasures, then she did not see a problem – even though she knew that Mick would see them more as vices.

"Okey dokey everyone – eyes down!"

The cringeworthy canned voice of the site heralded the start of a new game, and Linda was hoping for a big win. She had won £500 the previous week which left her with plenty of cash when combined with what Mick gave her. Of course, she would never tell him that such an event had occurred. Just as Linda started watching the coloured balls come up on the screen, the loud sound of metal on metal resounded from outside: the gate. Benny came back full of smiles running up the drive with Mick, just behind him, also smiling. Linda quickly forced the laptop shut, but it was still making irritating sounds as the virtual bingo caller enthusiastically read out the randomly generated numbers. She flicked a few latches up and down and yanked out what she believed to be the battery in a panicked frenzy to silence the laptop. It made a strange noise. There were still lights on it and the item she was holding was thin, encased in metal and had a small ribbon attached which she presumed must be for carrying, it looked too small to be the battery. Linda was never the most technical and was just grateful to have silenced the thing before Mick heard. Benny she could fob off, but Mick rarely missed a trick with anything like that.

"Mum!" Benny raced through the door and gave Linda a big hug. "We were losing but we got a last minuter, right in front of us! Mirallas pointed at me!"

Linda smiled at her son as he rushed upstairs to try and recreate the match on his Xbox 360 as he loved to do. Her head then turned to Mick, and the smile on her face disappeared as she spoke in a brusk tone.

"What exactly was that crap earlier? You call before you come here – you know that."

"You'd not answer if I rang and you know it. I've not seen the lad in a fortnight. I give you more than you'd get if we did this legally, can a father not take his lad to a bloody match? He'd forget who I am if you had it your way, maybe it's better if I just go through the courts, at least you couldn't play these stupid bloody games then."

"You do that and I'll see to it that you never see your son again, I'm warning you Michael!"

Mick grimaced as he and his wife looked at each other with nothing but pure hatred, contempt and loathing for one another. He replied in a calm, yet menacing tone. "If that's how you want to play it then so be it."

Mick wheeled around and went to walk to his car. He got halfway down the path, and then turned around in a moment akin to Columbo.

"But if I notice the booze and ciggies on the go, so will Social Services."

As Mick walked down the driveway, Linda was left stunned. She had thought herself quite the cover-up artist, and she was truly aghast to see how easily her actions had been noticed and flagged up by her husband. Mick gave a sarcastic wave as he got into his car: half for Benny to say goodbye as he waved out of his bedroom window, and half to wind Linda up. She stormed back in and slammed the door, which made a loud enough bang to scare nearby birds out of their trees.

Linda had decided that she may be as well hanged a martyr as tried one. She sat there that evening, knocking back the wines, irate at the day's events. Benny was engrossed in his game and would be for at least another two hours – probably more. Mick had taken him out for his tea, and she decided that her duties in serving her son were finished for the day. She turned the television back on.

The TV was still on the news channel. A new yellow breaking news bar was running along the bottom of the screen, stating that another body had been found in Twickenham, outside an old warehouse. It had been dumped in a disused industrial waste bin and was believed to have been there for some time. It had only been found on the investigation of a thick blanket of bluebottles that were covering the bin. No police confirmation had been given, but a supermarket manager had been missing for several weeks, after going on his lunch break one day and never coming back. One of the unfortunate souls who had opened the bin, to a swarm of angered bluebottles not too dissimilar to something from one of the Mummy series of films, was talking to a reporter. He was describing the body as severely mutilated – speculating that it had been there for some time, judging by the repugnant stench of putrefied flesh.

All of this was too depressing for Linda. She was sick of hearing about these murders that were still going on. She put it down to incompetent, bumbling police officers likely missing obvious clues. A strong stab of one of the rubber buttons on the power-weary remote changed the channel, and she saw that there was a reality TV show coming on. She knew that she should go and check on Benny, but she took for granted the fact that he would still be engrossed in his game. Her body was calling out for more booze, and she was only too happy to answer it. She mulled over the day's events as the glass became emptier. There was no way she was going to let Mick get the better of her. She focused on that thought as the programme started, adamant that she would not be beaten.

FOURTEEN

Roger did not have much passion for life left in him. He had been neglecting himself in order to complete his work. It took a lot of studying, a lot of planning and all of it weighed so heavily on his mind, both before and after the courtroom. He preferred to work away from home so as not to be recognised by previous offenders – though with the sentences he was known for dishing out it was unlikely a past offender would come into his life again.

Roger was sat in his flat watching the news. It focused on a body being found in Twickenham. He did not know much about the place other than it was where England played rugby – and he used to have a friend who always spoke about having seen Iron Maiden there in 2008, as though it were the defining moment of his life. Maybe it was exactly that for his old friend. Even the thought of that made Roger sad: his happiness had been taken away from him when his father passed away. *All so unnecessary, the lot of it,* but what was done was done now and could not be changed.

The very reason why Roger was trying to press on in his job and earn divine retirement was for his father. Such evil walked the streets. Beings that didn't even deserve the carbon-filled air they greedily sucked in each day, while those they had harmed could do nothing but rot beneath the ground – or blow in the wind, depending on their funeral preferences. As the newsreader continued to talk about the body that was found, Roger thought back to his visit to Twickenham, where he had passed a sentence some weeks earlier.

★ ★ ★

The defendant was more of a mollusc than a man: an invertebrate of the lowest form. The evidence against him was damning, as were almost all of the cases that Roger presided over. He dealt with some of the worst filth the world had to offer, and deemed it his duty in life in the hope that he would complete his penance on earth rather than purgatory. A snivelling figure grudgingly listened as his crimes were read out. He was found guilty of victimisation in the workplace and singling out hard-working individuals – making their lives a misery solely because he had not liked them. It was a constructive dismissal of sorts, but the unfortunate victim never got the chance to resign.

The wretch of a defendant stood at about roughly 6 foot 3 inches and wore grey trousers with a short sleeve shirt. The arms sticking out of the shirt were skeletal, with virtually no muscle mass. The legs may have been covered by the trousers, but they were likely to have been equally like that of a matchstick man if the body was in average proportion. Atop the head was hair akin to Sonic the Hedgehog and a set of gold-framed glasses sat upon the face, which maintained a permanently squinted expression. This particular defendant had not only protested his innocence but threatened the judge with further action, claiming that he would see to it that Roger would no longer be able to continue his profession. Roger did not think that he could be any more disgusted by this jumped-up store manager, but the slimy and effeminate way in which he had attempted to defend himself turned the judge's stomach.

He had been stood before Roger with his hands bound but had somehow managed to slip a hand free from his restraints. With that bony hand, he had struck the judge. It was more of a slap than a punch. The move had caught Roger completely off guard and caused him to lose his footing. It was fortunate that courts were most secure places. The defendant banged at the exit door in the hope it would give way. Judge Birch rose to his feet and dusted himself off. The pounding at the door had quickly become more desperate as Roger drew nearer. Blood was running down his cheek. Had the strike been a punch there would be no blood. The cowardly slap had been an attempt at a scratch. Unkempt nails had broken the skin on Roger's face. He abhorred men who let their nails grown long. He also abhorred men who fought like 'whores.'

The rhythm at which the defendants' fists were hammering, the door grew increasingly frantic. The court remained silent. There would be no interference. It was Roger's courtroom, and he would deal with every last detail of it. A scrawny hand once again flailed out at Roger. This time he saw the dirty move coming and caught the stick-thin arm, restraining it without the need for much effort. A scarecrow-like leg then flew out in a desperate attempt to hit the judge where it hurt. Roger again saw this move coming and seized the leg with his other arm. The restrained weasel of a store manager lost his balance. He sunk his fingers into the judge, gripping his clothing tightly, and the pair clattered to the concrete floor.

Roger attempted to get back to his feet straight away. He placed an arm on the floor for balance. He felt a bolt of pain surge through him. The floored defendant had bitten him. He had sunk his teeth right in – and had torn a small chunk out of the judge's forearm – like some kind of savage animal. High levels of pain can sometimes alleviate the mind of the limitations and frailties of the body – enable it to live in the moment for a short period. Roger was experiencing this phenomenon right there and then. He moved as fast as he had in his teenage years. He withdrew his right arm and punched the defendant in the face. The force of the punch made the head bounce off the concrete: double impact. Blood spurted all over the dusty concrete floor: Roger was leaking heavily: a chunk of flesh maintained its allegiance to the arm via a ribbon of skin.

The store manager already had a squint, but his glasses having been smashed worsened the comical facial expression – most likely due to small fragments of glass having gone into his eye. His visual aid was gone, yet still he flailed out at Roger's face. The judge struck him again and again. Roger felt the bony fingers upon his face: scratching against him, searching for his eyes, eventually finding them and attempting to claw against them.

Justice needed to be done. Roger would not let this criminal go free. He refused to let himself be bested by such a cheap and dirty move. This was surely contempt of court. He knew he may have to pass the sentence there and then without the usual procedure and ceremony that went with it.

The two meaty hands of the judge grasped the shoulders of the defendant and began to smash them back and forth against the floor. The head bounced off the concrete with a sickening sound. The thick bone of the skull began to give way from the impact where fissures would likely be forming beneath the skin. Roger then proceeded to punch the defendant across the face. Were it the days of Rome and were this instance to occur in the Colosseum, the crowd would have been going wild at such a spectacle. Six heavy blows. The defendant's body became limp – but not lifeless. Motor functions remained, but were operating at a critical level. Roger dragged him back across the floor to the middle of the courtroom. His crimes needed to be addressed and a sentence dealt.

An invisible fire burned in the judge's knuckles from the punishment he had dished out. Visible flames flickered in his eyes. Roger did not know if he had the strength to finish his term as a judge before his scheduled retirement. He endeavoured to do his best to get there: he had come too far to give up – *way too far indeed!* There was still quite a way to go on his journey, but the blessed release he hoped that he would experience at the end of it spurred him on. He imagined the calm, the release from the mental agony of which he was a chronic sufferer. He closed his eyes for a moment but then his vision of that peaceful island which he was desperate to visit was snatched away as the defendant groaned and tried to crawl his way along the ground. Roger remembered why he was where he was, what his job was. He read out the list of crimes as he passed the sentence, bringing the gavel down – again and again and again.

The news had taken Roger a couple of months back in time – to that case in January. It had been one of his first big challenges in the courtroom. It had taken place on unfamiliar territory. A cold winters' day in London had proved most testing, and all he had wanted to do after it was get back to home turf. He had caught the first train home, but not before stopping at a newsagent for a cheap bottle of no-name whisky which he concealed in his jacket and surreptitiously sipped during the journey. The feeling of returning home as the train pulled in to Lime Street had been a euphoric one for Roger. There was something about returning home that always made him feel better: it signified safety, sanctuary and familiarity. The trip had been a risk, but Roger was grateful that it had paid off. Sat watching the news that day in his flat, he knew he still had a few more cases to go. Roger was glad that he had a few cases behind him in the run up to his retirement. The sooner he got them out of the way the better.

FIFTEEN

The shrill tone of the breaking news jingle sounded, replacing the scheduled Merseytalk debate about hospital waiting times. On the television, a yellow banner ran across every regional channel in the Merseyside area, informing viewers that a police warning had been issued. An almighty hangover had meant that there was no chance of Linda turning on the TV that day and she was paying the radio little attention – it was all a great din to her as she lay on the sofa, wishing with all her might that the feeling of an 18-wheel lorry speeding along a pothole-laden path within her mind would disappear. Three empty bottles of Jacob's Creek Chardonnay consumed the previous evening had been the cause of her ailments, but she had decided to give herself a little treat – an attempt to make herself feel a little better after the events which had transpired that afternoon.

Mick had been on the phone, screaming at his wife. Linda had finally pushed him too far in his ongoing endeavours to see his son. He had been easy going: he had tried to let things settle and sort things out amicably, solely because he wanted matters to be as relaxed for Benny as possible. The final straw had been when Linda denied Mick the chance to see his son on the lad's ninth birthday. It was an act which had left Mick seething and had awakened a hate-filled part of him that he never knew existed until that moment. It begged to take over his mind, promising him divine release if he permitted it just a moment's control. He had tried to ward the temptation away, but Linda had continued to goad the beast within, and eventually she incited it to the point where Mick could no longer contain it.

After being repeatedly fobbed off when trying to arrange access to his son, Mick had turned up unannounced for Benny's birthday. It was an attempt at a pleasant surprise for his lad. And an effort to thwart his wife's devious ways, after she had used virtually every excuse and trick in the book to keep her husband at arms length. One of her favourites was pretending to be out, despite the fact that Mick knew full well that she rarely went anywhere. She used to like to watch him from the window as he stood, angrily stabbing his mobile keypad, trying to get through to her: a call she would never pick up. She thought that he looked pathetic, and it was a thought which never failed to give her the beginnings of a smirk. The smug grin was wiped off her face on Benny's birthday.

A seething Mick managed to trick her and finally have his say. He had gone to a neighbours' house feigning concern for his wife's well-being. Carelessly, she had answered her phone. She saw on the screen that it was Frank and Frances calling from down the road. They never usually called unless there was a problem. Linda was furious that she had not considered this *before* picking up the call. Mick had yelled and bawled at her, letting his wife know how he felt regarding her abhorrent attitude towards him. During the brief call, in which he did most of the speaking, he called her a host of four letter words and told her in no uncertain terms that she would regret her actions and that he would see her in court – a cliché which carried with it a finality when used from one partner to another in a withering relationship: the crumbling wall slumping beyond all repair.

Frank and Frances had eventually pulled the cord on the phone and consoled Mick, as he fell to the floor in tears following the impromptu cut-off. Less than a mile up Acacia Avenue, Linda was smirking. The insidious grin had replaced a scowl when she realised the state her soon-to-be-ex husband had gotten into. She took delight in the knowledge that he was suffering.

The run up to Benny's birthday had frustrated Linda. The boy was asking hundreds of questions about his dad. She was just about sick of it. Just because Mick took him to football matches and fast food restaurants, Benny thought his dad was God. With that in mind, Linda was intent on committing deicide. She wanted Mick to be a fallen idol, not a revered one. She told Benny that Mick would not be coming on his birthday because he was too busy. To a young lad turning nine-years-old, who had always had his dad in his life, it was heartbreaking. He had spent most of the day in the isolation of his bedroom, only coming down for his cake when called. Linda sang him happy birthday. Even though she had ensured his absence from the day's proceedings, Mick still managed

78

to throw a spanner in the works when it came to presents.

Benny had wanted the most recent Everton kit. All of his friends at school had it, and were laughing at him for still having last season's issue – a mindset manufacturers had gone to great lengths to instil in the vast majority of young boys: the days of scarves and team colours being enough were long gone. Linda had little interest in football, and her lack of knowledge had been to her detriment, as Benny's face evidenced, when he removed the wrapping paper containing what he thought would be his new shirt. It turned out to be a training top – not the official first team replica shirt. Almost as expensive, but worthless in terms of status among peers to a young boy. Benny had ended up in tears. His dad would have known which one to get him. Voicing that got him a thorough telling-off for ingratitude, and he was sent to bed early – on the one night of the year he was usually allowed to stay up late.

Following her sons outburst, Linda had remained sat downstairs, with minimal lighting. Benny's crying had eventually ceased. She presumed he must have fallen asleep and was grateful for the opportunity to get more wine into her system. After several glasses of chardonnay, Linda wondered if the booze had gone straight to her head: she put the radio on, and the news appeared to have replaced the usual Seventies at Seven. It was claiming that the Neo Ripper had made his way back up north – back up to Merseyside. The semi-pulped remains of a man had been found dumped down a Formby alleyway in a rubble sack. A betting shop worker had been smoking by the side of the shop and received the shock of her life, as she peeked into a random blue bag in an effort to see what was inside that was attracting so many rats and flies in broad daylight. Police had issued a warning for the residents of Formby and surrounding areas: stay indoors where possible. The body was much fresher than previous cadavers: *they believed the killer could still be in the area.*

Linda had passed out during the news. Upon waking, her stomach turned for a moment, as she realised it was not a dream brought on by an excess of wine as first she had thought. She remembered how bad she had felt when a murder had taken place over the water, but such an event occurring just a short drive away in Formby was unthinkable. With the police warning confirming in no uncertain terms that danger lurked nearby, she felt like she might pass out again but this time from a sickening level of fear and panic. The only link police were able to draw between the killings, despite months of research and investigation, was the gruesome way in which their bodies were tortured – whilst still alive. Linda hated anything gory, dark or macabre, and she was always scared of her old job coming back to haunt her. After all the efforts she had made in the name of self progression, she truly had destroyed more than a few lives with her decisions. The radio had a simple one-touch switch to turn it off, but Linda yanked the plug out of the wall – detaching the socket from the plasterboard, such was the level of force she used. It looked effective in the movies, but US plugs flew out easier than the British standard. Her rash action caused the circuit-breaker fuses to trip in the house. Her world was literally plunged into darkness: it was the last thing she wanted at that moment. She staggered to the fusebox as quickly as she could, desperate to eradicate this darkness.

★ ★ ★

The lack of focus from the hangover did not stop Linda from thinking about that which terrified her. A New Brighton doctor, a youth in North Wales, a supermarket manager in London and now a member of Sefton Council had all found themselves victims of the Neo Ripper. Linda tried to reiterate to her mind that if she were a target, she would have been dead by now – though such mental efforts did little to comfort her. Wherever the killer was, the police would get him – of that she was sure. Despite her endeavours to quell her mental anguish, Linda was unable to stop her hands from trembling, attributable to a combination of the lack of alcohol in her system and her nerves. She had not eaten anything that morning because she felt so ill, but she knew that liquid aid in the form of a hair of the dog would help. Shuffling to the kitchen and opening Mick's prized bottle of single malt – made all the more appealing by the fact he saved it for special occasions – she filled a tumbler halfway and gulped it down in one go. Instant relief. Another half tumbler was poured and again downed. Benny still needed to be woken up and prepared for school. She did not want to leave the house, but neither did she want her boy missing out on his education. His results and grades were too important to risk as far as she was concerned. Sefton schools remained open whilst those in the Southport area were all closed; the decision made little sense, but bizarre decisions were all too common within the education system since the year 2000. Linda was glad that the school was within walking distance, because she was in no fit state to drive. She may have risked it if it was just her travelling, but she would never put her son's safety at risk. He was everything to her. Linda put the car keys in a drawer, just so she would not be tempted. The police warning was still present in her mind, but she had inadvertently put it right at the back for the time being. Her head felt like there was a pile driver rumbling away inside it, and that took precedence against all else. She knelt down and gave Benny's hair a smoothing with her hand, before straightening the tie that made up part of his school uniform. She took her son's hand, and they ventured out together beneath a grey and cloudy sky.

SIXTEEN

An enraged man beat his fists against one of the walls of his abode, until the thin layer of skin over his knuckles split open. Each punch added crimson sprays to the yellowed walls of a severely aged bedsit, creating a chilling form of abstract art. The coffee table had been kicked over, sending all manner of papers and two mugs onto the floor. The mugs smashed, and the dregs of coffee that were in them spread across the ancient green carpet that had once been the pinnacle of style in the 1970s.

The television also found itself the victim of a boot. Modern flat-screens would not have stood a chance, but this was an old-style CRT with glass screen: a 32-inch behemoth, which stood firm when attacked and left its assailant with a throbbing pain in his foot. Enduring the stomach-churning pain of a fractured toe, the man hobbled over to an old shoebox full of tools in an electrical cupboard near the front door and sought out a hammer – it was not quite as old as the carpet, but the years had added spots of rust and paint to it. The man limped back over to the television, wincing with each step.

News was showing on the screen which he did not care one jot for: he had turned the set on in the hope of a programme or movie, but instead every channel had been rolling news. A hammer blow to the face of the reporter caused little damage other than a small crack. Two more frantic whacks, and the thick glass screen began to give way – but *still* it had plenty of fight left in it. The hammer was then turned on its side to give a better surface area to assault – all that did was take most of the force away from the attack. Such an assault on an inanimate object may have seemed like the action of a man hanging desperately to the frayed ends of sanity, but after the initial strike, an inability to complete the intended destruction enraged the seething individual all the more, amplifying the fury caused by his self doubt. Intent on finishing what he started, the man placed the sole of the boot of his non-injured foot against the top of the unit and sent the television off its stand. Now lying flat, it was susceptible to the stronger blows from above, and with a frenzied series of bangs, the screen eventually gave way as a few sparks flew, a blueish smoke emanating from the hole. In a modern house, the circuit breakers would have tripped, but the wiring in the edifice was ancient, with red, black and green insulating sleeves still in place instead of the brown, blue and the striped earth colourings of more modern wiring.

Michael Painter was a man who had reached his limit. Being denied access to his son by his mendacious harpy of a wife was crippling him far more than the fracture in his foot ever could. She had made the matter tediously difficult for him already, in the short space of time they had been apart, but the birthday incident had sent Mick into a frenzy that *he* did not think was possible for him to get into. He was, generally, a mild-mannered man who got on with most people, and the only time he was seen angry was when Everton played badly. The Mick who stood in his Litherland bedsit, with every muscle and sinew twitching, was a different man entirely.

★ ★ ★

Frank and Frances had tried to console Mick, as he broke down in tears and fell to his knees following the phone call. He had left the car in Crosby, bought himself a bottle of cheap Scotch whisky at a small convenience store and made his way home – in a half-hearted shuffle that matched how he felt inside. There was a bag of presents in the car, but he seriously doubted that they would ever get to be given to his boy. Mick felt so lost and confused that he was not quite sure of what planet he was actually on. It was the type of state that only a severe shock to the nerves can get a man into.

The convenience store had been one of those where the entire shop is hidden behind a wall of plastic, and any desired items are provided by the attendant via a small hole – but only after cash has changed hands. To Mick, the thick plastic walls may as well have been padded. He felt he was going crazy, and that was before he had even opened the Scotch. He had slugged a good half of it on the way back, taking shortcuts through areas he would normally avoid due the likely presence of gangs of young slobs, but on that day he did not care who he ran into: he would be immune to anything they could throw at him, verbally or physically.

Mick did not come across any gangs on the way home, but outside his dilapidated block of flats there were the usual gang of shaven headed teenage deadbeats, kicking a football menacingly in his direction. It bounced off the wall he was passing several times, and he was not sure whether they had been aiming for him and missing or were just trying to make the ball bounce close to him in an effort to rile him up. Mick knew that if it was the latter, they need not have wasted their energy: he was already fully charged in that department. He walked on, not in the mood for any kind of interaction with anyone, but a few members of the group could not contain themselves and shouted to him.

"Ey mate, will ya get us some ciggies from the shop?"

"Giz a bit of that whisky there mate!"

Normally Mick at least acknowledged them – if only in an effort to save future hassle – but on that occasion he walked up the steps without saying a word. He was not a big drinker, but the impact of the whisky had hit him, and his inhibitions were lessened: the desired effect had been achieved, and that was the reason he had bought it.

Mick had been in a daze most of the way home, but as the shock of everything wore off, hatred found some cracks in his resolve and soon flooded its way in, engulfing his mind like a tsunami. The news had beckoned it, and he was trying every way that he could to free his mind of the insatiable anger because of it: smashing stuff seemed to do just that. The news had reported that the 'Neo Ripper' had returned to Merseyside. Mick and Linda had not been the happiest for some time, but that murder over the water had been what started the avalanche of their break up. Mick was adamant that it would not have happened so soon otherwise. Even the bedsit was symbolic: the reason he was living in a pokey dump, instead of his grand detached home in Crosby, was because of his vile specimen of a wife.

He had initially intended to fight for both custody of Benny and the house, but he knew that the courts always worked in the woman's favour – even in cases where they were clearly the ones in the wrong. Smashing the place up had felt good – a release – especially silencing the television, which was serving as an all too unwelcome reminder of where his woes started. His beast mode may have subsided for a moment, and he was no longer screaming at a television, but Mick's mind was still in overdrive. He knew how things were going to pan out with Linda: she would take away the one thing he loved most, his son. He knew that the custody battle would last at least a year, maybe two, and that his wife would use every trick in the book against him. Mick knew how Linda worked: she would moan, cry and act all innocent, whilst insisting that what was best for Benny was stability at home. Social services would fall for her ruse, and Mick knew he would not have a legal leg to stand on.

There was no going back after the birthday incident. A thought crossed his mind that he could not even entertain for more than a millisecond: the idea of getting back with Linda. Just thinking about it made him shudder. The way time flew, Benny would soon be a teenager, and the last thing Mick wanted in his boy's life was constant arguments. Linda had drawn a line in the sand with the birthday fiasco, and Mick was buried up to his neck at the very point in which the tide threatened to overwhelm him. He was not about to let that happen. If he was to drown then he would take the wicked witch down with him. His unstable mind stifled a laugh at the idea of Linda rising out of the water on a broomstick, as true witches were said to be able to do in days gone by. He would not put it past her.

Thousands of bleak and hopeless thoughts swirled through Mick's mind at the same time; he was quite literally seeing red as his inner thoughts became clouded with both rage and alcohol. Several ideas rattled around in his head. One of them stood out more than the rest, and though he searched through others, he kept coming back to that same one. The fact that the thought had come to Mick had actually frightened him as to just how badly he felt towards his wife – so much so that he lay back on the bed for a moment in an effort to gather his thoughts. The stress of the day had worn him out and closing his eyes briefly brought on instant sleep.

Upon waking, the same thought which had troubled Mick remained in his mind. *She* had to go. An end had to be put to his personal nightmare, before it worsened further. He took a gulp of whisky, straight from the bottle, and picked up the hammer which he had dropped among the shards of glass that had been his TV screen. The tool felt good in his hand. Without a second thought, he made his way back out the front door – snatching up the bottle of whisky from the floor, which had somehow avoided getting smashed whilst he had been going berserk. Mick felt strong, almost as though he was possessed by some celestial spirit which was empowering him. A spirit was indeed contributing to this, but not a celestial one: the no-name whisky, 'Foggy Glen,' was certainly proving good value-for-money.

Mick marched out of the door and down the steps with a look on his face which would discourage anyone with half a brain cell from even *thinking* about getting in his way, let alone causing him a problem. In one hand, he held a bottle; in the other, he wielded a hammer. It had been dark when he had come home, but the sky had turned crimson since his sleep. He presumed that he must have been asleep for most of the following day. The gang were outside his building again, and they could not but save themselves from shouting something yet again, engaging in the most interesting thing they had seen all day. One of them called out in a quizzical, bet-you-wouldn't tone.

"Ya gonna smash someone's head in with that, mate?"

Again, Mick did not bother to reply despite the hor-rifically ironic enquiry. More shouts were heard as he carried on walking, several insults too. On a normal day, he would have given the group a piece of his mind, con-fronting the leader – but there and then, he had total tunnel vision, and his hearing was tuned to a frequency they could not hope to invade.

Setting off across Rimrose Valley Park, Mick knew exactly what he intended to do, and believed that if it was not meant to be, then God or some divine being would intervene. God must have approved – or been too busy – because Mick got all the way to his former abode without hindrance. He had been travelling in the early hours of the evening, when the items in his hand were still visible in the fading daylight. Several police cars had passed him, but not one of them stopped him. The priority was to find the allegedly-nearby killer. Mick found it almost laughable as he made his pilgrimage of vengeance that despite the current state of emergency, no police seemed to pay any attention to a man walking along with a hammer in one hand and a bottle in the other. He gathered that they probably saw him as an alcoholic, and that their eyes had focused on the bottle more than the tool-come-weapon. The bread and butter of local policing had altered considerably in recent years. Hate crimes and domestic violence incidents were seen as a greater priority than assaults and robberies, but with a serial killer apparently running loose in Merseyside, the entire force had a serious hard-on for the action that was to come.

Mick stood beneath the yellow hued streetlights of Acacia Avenue, looking at the house where once his life had seemed so perfect. Darkness had fallen. The entire avenue was silent. There was not a soul in sight. The light in Benny's room was off. Mick was unsure of the time, but knew that it was late. His boy would most likely be fast asleep. The living room light was not on, but there was a source of distant illumination passing through the living room window. Linda would be in the kitchen. She would often retreat there after arguments – mainly because it provided her with easy access to her wine, which she was all too enamoured with.

Mick still had a small amount of whisky left in his bottle. He had swallowed most of it on the way, but there was about an eighth left. Mick raised the green Foggy Glen bottle to his mouth and gulped what was left in one go. He had not drank in such a manner since he was in his teens. He went to imitate the show-off action of his teens, by smashing it on the floor via a hard throw – it was as though his brain still retained its programming from all those years past. The action had not impressed any potential girlfriends back then, and Mick knew that it would not help him now, so he deposited the bottle in a random wheelie bin. As he turned back towards his marital home, he saw the silhouette of the Medusa which caused his fist to clench more tightly around the wooden handle of the lump hammer.

It was time to do what needed to be done.

SEVENTEEN

It had taken Roger a good few weeks to get over the last trial. His fists hurt more than he remembered them doing so when he had ended up in a few scrapes in his youth. Forties were meant to be the new thirties, they said, but as he was nearing a half century, he felt that such a statement held less credence than it was given by modern society. His back ached, and his knees were sore, from having knelt on the concrete floor for so long. There was a lesion on his face from where he had been scratched. There were deep grazes around his neck from where the defendant had resisted. Roger knew he should have been resting and leading a healthy lifestyle to try and get back to full fitness; instead, he spent most nights slumped in a chair in his city centre apartment, downing Rebel Fire bourbon and watching from his window as the lights of a city-centre night swayed like ocean waves. He had gone out a few times for food, sometimes for the company of the mass population, so as not to be alone, or other times just because he could not take being within the four walls of his apartment anymore.

Despite the troubles that his profession brought him, Roger had kept his living space in good condition. It was modern and had been built following the construction surge Liverpool enjoyed after acting as the European Capital of Culture in 2008. He had returned there after many a court case, glad of somewhere to stay. He found it very therapeutic most of the time, though not as much as walks down Crosby promenade. When his offer had been accepted on the property, he was still in his thirties, and life still held much promise. He had spent many years as a teacher prior to his career as a judge, teaching law to secondary school students. The amount of gaps, grey areas and loopholes had always appalled him – as well as the pitiful sentences dished to those he believed deserved far worse. The death of his father had caused him to pursue his new-found career. Judge Birch was not a fan of second chances or going easy on those who had committed heinous crimes.

Almost a month of recuperation from the previous case had given Roger plenty of time to gather information on what would serve as his penultimate one. He had known that it would be a very personal case. He was also wise enough to know that he should not let his feelings get in the way of justice, but he felt that both matters ran on parallel roads and would wind up at the same destination at some point along the way.

Roger could not remember much about his mother, but his dad had spoken about her every single day of his life. At the time of his wife's death, Billy Birch could not afford a headstone for her final resting place in Thornton cemetery. He did not want to purchase a wooden cross, as he had heard tales of thefts and wanted something that would stand the test of time. After many years of leaving flowers on the patch of grass, which the body of his wife lay beneath, Billy had decided to create his own memorial. He believed there was far greater sentiment behind such an act. He had initially been told such things were not permitted in the gardens of rest, but he saw graves with family photos propped up on them, children's graves with prams and balloons next to them and even tinsel put around headstones at Christmas. He had taken some time to pick out decorative chains and placed them in a rectangle on his late wife's plot. Within the chains he had planted pansies and lined the border with blue and white lobelia. They were both his wife's favourite flowers, and she loved colour in her garden. Lastly, he had added a wooden stake with an engraved plaque atop it which read

'Annie Birch, 1935–1978. Forever young.'

Billy had been emotional but very proud of his efforts. After being ripped off via fraud, he knew that he would not be able to save up enough money for a headstone in the time he had left on the planet, but in his older years he had made it his mission to do *something* for his wife so that her grave would not be forgotten and combined with others in a mass grave after approximately 50 years – a custom regulation of which few people were aware.

Just over a fortnight later, Billy had returned to find his hard work not only undone, but totally decimated. There were holes where the stakes that held the chains had once been. The recently planted flowers had been ruthlessly yanked out of the ground with remnants of leaf and stalk still visible. Even the wooden post with the plaque was gone. At first, Billy was certain that youths were to blame: the slob culture of the modern day had reached a new extreme. He had not cared that he was old – he would find them and make them answer for what they had done. He marched over to the gravekeeper's hut to ask if there were any cameras that could help him. The man in the hut looked embarrassed when questioned, like a child that knows something but is incapable of managing their facial expressions to hide it.

When he was told that the council had removed his hand crafted memorial, Billy was left aghast. The gravekeeper explained that he was only there for general maintenance: throwing away dead flowers, deterring youths and keeping the area in good condition. He informed a stunned Billy that it was in fact the council who had come and removed the memorial. The crushing blow came as he saw a skip outside the cemetery on his way out. In the skip was a pile of turf, some general rubbish, a few black bin bags and – on top of it all – were the remains of what had been a simple, yet beautiful, memorial. Upon protest to the council, Billy was shot down and informed, in a manner most cold, that his makeshift memorial did not adhere to health and safety guidelines. He enquired as to how other items in the graveyard could remained untouched, and was again reminded of health and safety guidelines. He was advised to purchase a headstone which met council guidelines, which he could not afford: even the cheapest would set him back a four-figure sum.

Out of all the things that occurred in the lead up to Billy Birch's death, the Nazi-like removal of his handmade memorial to his beloved wife was possibly the most painful injustice suffered. The cancer which the doctor had missed would get him eventually: he could deal with that. A devious man from a foreign land had stolen all the money he had left: he had dealt with that. But old Billy had broken down in tears at the way the council had dealt with him over a no-frills memorial for his dear wife.

Throughout much of his suffering, Billy had kept matters to himself. Roger sat in a small coffee shop on Dale Street, musing to himself about what could have been. If his father had just told him some of the things that were going on, then he could have intervened earlier – perhaps he would not be in the situation he was now had his old dad not been so proud. He knew that could never have been the case. People were built differently in the previous generation: they had endured a war and years of poverty after it as the country struggled to get back onto its feet. Roger had gone to visit the memorial to his mother, once: the week it was done. He had returned again a month later and seen it was gone. He had gone to see his dad straight away about it, and that was the only time Roger could ever recall seeing a tear in his dad's eye.

"Dad?" He had asked in that caring fashion that represents a hundred ways of asking if somebody is alright without actually asking it. Billy's lip had quivered. Without another word being spoken, Roger embraced his dad – who returned the gesture strongly.

"I give up – ya know, son – I really do!" Roger held his dad tightly, consoling him and feeling pure hatred for the injustices his dear father had suffered. He had stared up at a photograph of the family together: an infant Roger, Billy with jet-black hair and his mother, Annie, so beautiful and so happy. Roger knew his dad did not have long left, and it was at that moment he had decided that he would avenge him one day – but not so soon that his dad would have to endure seeing his son sent to prison. Roger believed that everyone would find their calling one day in life, and as he sat in Mersey Coffees, his mind had recalled what lead him to his calling. He had sat in a daze, remembering all that went on in the run up to losing his father. He went through it all upon waking each and every day and prior to sleeping – when he was able to sleep.

Roger was relieved to have dealt with the council chief – the one who had ultimately made the decision to literally rip the memorial from the ground and speak to his dad like dirt over the phone. This particular species of vermin had crumbled straight away in the courtroom. In prior meetings, he had been the big 'I am' – belittling and threatening Roger that he would call the police. When Lawrence Beasley had made the threats, he had not realised that he was dealing with the law himself, and that anything he did and said would *most definitely* be used against him in a court of law – though in his courtroom, Roger was the one who decided *what* constituted a fair trial.

★ ★ ★

Lawrence could not remember how he got into a dusty old shell of a building, but when he awoke he recognised the face of the man in front of him – it was the same man who had confronted him a few days earlier about his mother's grave. Lawrence struggled and felt a surge of pain run through him as he tried to free his hands from behind his back. A cold voice gave him some unwanted information, confirming to the council chief that the situation in which he had found himself was every bit as bad as he had imagined it to be.

"Barbed wire for you. I'm all out of handcuffs." Roger stood, dressed all in black, wearing a leather duster. He looked like something out of an old western – to the man kneeling before him, Judge Birch appeared truly terrifying.

"I don't know what I've supposedly done to you – but please, just let me go. I've got a family!"

The defendant sobbed. Since Roger had been a judge, he had got used to defendants' crying and sobbing, but he had never heard any like this before. It was false – an act.

"Silence please: court is now in session." Roger paced around the defendant in a circle, striding slightly slower in his blind spot so as to amplify the nerves of his 'victim' to be. Roger did not see the man in his courtroom as a 'victim': that word had connotations of innocence, and this man certainly did not possess anything of the sort; of that Roger was sure.

"You say you do not know who I am. I am the son of William and Annie Birch – do *those* names ring a bell to you? Do you remember what you did to *them*?" Roger's voice rasped as he finished his question.

Truly petrified at that moment, Lawrence was unable to think straight. He tried to reply to the stern-faced judge standing before him but merely let out a staccato stammer of gibberish as his lips and tongue moved – no coherent words were formed. He bowed his head and looked at the floor, trying to regain some focus and possibly find a way out of this hell he had been thrust into. The attempt did not last more than a few seconds, as the judge grabbed a fistful of hair and snapped the defendants head back – forcing him to look at a photograph held in a meaty hand.

"Are you telling me that you *do not* remember this man?!" Roger spat as he barked out the question – an irate shout that resounded throughout the disused factory.

Lawrence could do nothing other than look at the photograph but it meant nothing to him: it could have been anyone. He had worked in various offices during his time with Sefton Council and made quite a career for himself, rising the ranks and kicking a few people down on his way up the mountain of management. Then, of course, there were the numerous residents who he had argued with. Many complaints had been made about him over the years, but when this happened he generally got moved to a different department.

When he had been moved to Births, Marriages and Deaths, the biggest problem he had foreseen was paperwork. It had been during a meeting regarding vandalism of Thornton cemetery that he had upset the wrong person, making a foolish error which would later cost him his life. The meeting had taken place in a small reception room at the side of the church. Council, clergy, police and relatives of those whose graves had been damaged were in attendance. The meeting had gone well and it had been the usual string of promises from a police force which was facing tremendous budget cuts at the same time as increasing levels of demand from the public. On his way out, Lawrence was surveying the graveyard. In the distance, out of the corner of his eye, he saw a very different grave. Upon closer inspection, it looked very nice: a hand-made memorial – but if somebody were to trip on the chains, then it would be a health-and-safety nightmare. That was one factor in the decision Lawrence would come to regret most profoundly – the other was that he just felt like throwing his weight around because he liked power and having others listen to him. He got off on it.

Lawrence had been *nothing* for the majority of his life. Picked on at school because he was a telltale, shunned throughout his work because he was a brown-nose, Lawrence loved that he had managed to get himself into a position where he could punish people. He saw to it that several of his colleagues got sacked along the way in order for him to attain promotion. He enjoyed the fact that people were forced to show him respect if they valued their jobs. He could have turned a blind eye to the memorial and maintained a respect for the dead; instead, he had marched straight to the gravekeeper's hut and given him a thorough telling-off for not having reported it. As soon as Lawrence got back to the office, he organised that the memorial be removed, as a priority, by the local maintenance team – and demanded that they comb the entire graveyard for anything else which breached regulations.

That display of power had ensured that he received several anonymous postal threats, got called some foul names over the phone and even told, in one email, that God would judge him. Those actions had little impact on how he slept at night, but finding himself knelt in a position similar to a man deep in prayer, whilst bound by barbed wire, had put the fear of God into him. It was not God judging him though – the kind and merciful God of the New Testament was nowhere to be seen, some Old Testament style wrath was raining down upon him. Lawrence was convinced that he must be in hell – that the self-proclaimed judge standing before him was indeed Satan. He had feared someone attacking him one day, but never dreamed anything like this could happen. He was living a nightmare.

As the slightly crumpled photograph was held before his eyes, Lawrence was unable to recall who the man standing in it was. His mind had raced through thousands of thoughts in an instant. He was disoriented – and for a second, he had lost focus, in that crazy moment becoming completely oblivious as to the gravely perilous situation that he was in. A lengthy silence was broken, as a white light flashed across his eyes, and a powerful strike made contact with his cheek. The cold voice began to bellow.

"You know why you *don't* know who this man is? Because *you* never even gave him the time of day. Filth like you – sat in an office telling my father how he should go about honouring his wife, my mother. Not even a chance to alter the memorial – no. Just vulgar destruction. You didn't just destroy the final craft of a dying man though – *you crushed his heart.*"

It all suddenly came flooding back to Lawrence. An old guy had kept calling the office. He had got through once and gave Lawrence an earful, so he had made a note of the number and told the receptionist fob him off in future. One time the old guy had even turned up at the office, and he had pretended not to be in. The man had pleaded, he just wanted to know why his memorial was removed so crudely. Lawrence had maintained a stone-wall approach though, viewing him as a woolly-headed old fool who did not have the capacity to understand health and safety – an old fossil that would give up eventually. Old Billy Birch had gone away back then, but Lawrence was feeling sick to the stomach in the court-room. He realised that his actions had come back to haunt him. Karma, comeuppance – however one may define it, Lawrence was soon to be a recipient of it. He attempted to beg for his life.

"P-please, it wasn't me – my fault, I mean. There's rules: if someone had fell, I'd have been sued. My life would've been finished. I've got a family."

"LIAR!" Roger yelled out, and that white flash returned again to the defendant's vision, as another strike was dealt to his face. Roger had big hands and knew how to use them, even though they still hurt from the previous case.

"You ignored him; you even hid from him: he saw you in the office that day and you scurried out of view like a cockroach fleeing from the light."

"I- I... I didn't know what to say: there's rules – r-r-regulations. Oh please, let me go: I've got a wife; I've got kids."

Judge Birch picked up a long-handled sledgehammer he had brought with him among other tools for the job. He was a meticulous planner: the defendant was bound to the floor, his wrists tied behind his back with razor-sharp barbed-wire that cut into his skin. The wire was secured to a metal loop that was bolted into the floor; it was not there by chance: Roger had installed it there in preparation for this case.

Lawrence was already in tremendous pain, but the sight of that hammer filled him with terror – a spectacle which the puddle of urine forming around his knees made clear. He tried with all his might to flee, causing the barbed wire to tighten to an excruciating level, slicing into his flesh like butter and causing him to collapse in a heap. The act enabled the defendant to loosen a hand, but Roger clocked on immediately. He was taking no chances after the last incident: there was *no way* he was going to have another runaway.

He charged at the defendant and raised the hammer as the defendant wriggled and flailed like a fish out of water. The judge twice brought the hammer down in the knee vicinity – and missed. The third attempt at a twice-unsuccessful action can be a curious one, often providing success with little scientific reason as to why. Roger pondered this theory as his third strike did indeed land, and a piercing cry rented the silent air of the old Johnson's factory. Another soon followed, as the second knee was seen to: this time a direct hit on the kneecap.

"You're going *nowhere*. You will stand trial and you **WILL** pay for your actions – oh, you *will pay indeed!*"

The screams continued throughout the early hours as Judge Birch examined the available evidence and passed the appropriate sentence. There was a moment of silence, when the defendant had passed out from pain, right around the time that fingers had begun to be removed with a set of chain cutters. Roger was ever the innovator and had several implements to hand in order to dish out the sentence he had passed: pliers, screwdrivers, a soldering iron – and a whole lot more items that had been invented and devised with household jobs in mind. His personal favourite was his hammer. He was a judge after all, and a judge needed a gavel. The screams following this sentence were extra loud. Though Roger was almost ready to retire, he knew that he had to be careful not to make foolish mistakes at this stage. Fortunately for the judge, there were other late night screams going on that night. A big argument was taking place between several people nearby, probably gangs in North Park, and the shouting and commotion were drowning out any noise disturbance that his courtroom was creating. The noise carried on for a considerable period – as did Judge Birch.

Roger hated being a judge: he took no pleasure in

what he did, but he did feel a great sense of relief every time he achieved justice against those who had wronged his father. He did not see his actions as revenge, either – in his mind, it was justice in its *purest* form, and he was the judge who *ensured* it was served.

When the defendant finally fell silent following his judgement – lacking any signs of life – Judge Birch placed what was left of him into a thick plastic rubble sack. Quite a mess had been made, and a few rats had already taken an interest from afar. Roger was always one step ahead, if not two: he grabbed the spade that he had brought with him and shovelled rubble and dirt all over the bloody, sticky stains. It was not the thorough job he normally did, but he knew there was not long left of this work. Soon he would be out of the profession – and if all his work was uncovered as he imagined it may be one day, he wanted to be well away from it all. There was no way he would go to jail for doing what he believed was right. He had a vision in his head of walking into a bar, similar to the ones in the city centre that him and his dad used to go. His dad would be there, betting-slips in hand and pint on the table. "Hello, old son." His dad would say. Life would continue as it should have done before the world drove his dad to an early death.

As he exited the factory that had served as his court-room for the evening, he was shocked for a moment as blue lights flashed and sirens wailed close by. For one sickening moment he thought that he may not make it to retirement. Fortune favoured him yet again: the ar-gument that he had overheard in the distance before sounded like it had turned into an all-out brawl. There was a roar coming from somewhere nearby that could only be the roar of battle, a fight taking place. Yells, grunts, pleas for mercy and all manner of the foulest language and jeers could be heard. The entire police force would be on it, which left Roger free to enjoy plain sailing as he drove his Ford Escort van out of Bootle, towards the Formby bypass and along Three Tuns Lane, with the bagged remnants of the late defendant in the back.

There was a large bin outside the betting shop that he knew was collected once a fortnight – a fact he learnt via an overheard conversation whilst surveying the council officer in the gambling establishment. He had laughed at how easy it was to discover information. Roger had found out online that Lawrence lived in Formby. The Sefton Council website and his profile even had a clear recent picture. It only took a day of hanging around the town centre until he saw the man who he was desperate to have a quiet word with, and personally inform of his court summons. Roger had followed him into the betting shop and hung around, placing a few small stakes on greyhound races and watching Lawrence put fifty-pound-note after fifty-pound-note into the roulette terminals. It always hurt going to a betting shop without his dad, but in that instance it was necessary if he was to achieve justice for the man's memory and legacy.

Whilst near the counter, he had heard the manager furiously sound off about the cleaner not depositing the bags of rubbish into the bin because they had lost the key. The manager had also expressed his fury that they could not even tell if the cleaner was doing his job properly, as the cameras were not working – and the technicians would not be able to arrive for another week. With that information, Roger was able to bring the court case forward considerably, which meant he would have to cut his respite between cases short. He intended to seize his chance in that window of opportunity and ensure that his defendant answer their summons as soon as possible. Roger did not have to wait long. Councillor Beasley showed up at the betting shop that very same evening.

Dawn was nearing, and the moon hid behind the clouds of a dark Merseyside sky as Roger pulled up alongside the Flying Farmer pub. With some difficulty, he hurled a heavy duty refuse sack into the pile of black bags which the betting shop cleaner had left next to the dumpster; it was thicker and a slightly deeper black than the rest but it blended enough so as not to attract attention from afar. Roger's eavesdropping had paid off. The sack made a loud, wet thud – similar to the sound a wellington makes when traversing a mud-laden field. He went to return to his car, but stopped dead in his tracks when he saw that there was a man sitting in a doorway right next to the bin. He mentally chastised himself for such a foolish error: his work was not yet complete, and this could have ruined it all. He had not noticed the figure in the darkness. Roger's streak of good fortune continued. Further inspection revealed that the man in the alcove was dressed in dirty, tatty clothes. He had a large bottle of vodka next to him and was completely passed out, jaw hanging open, revealing a small selection of crooked, yellowed teeth. Roger's heart had almost stopped when he first saw the rough sleeper, but he drove away content that he had not been seen. He could have dealt with the man, but he was not about to go around killing those who he did not view as being on trial. Even if they were unlikely to be missed by anyone, he was someone's family and had caused Roger no harm.

His chest continued to hurt on the drive back home. It had hurt a lot in recent years, even more so since he had become a judge. Heart problems ran in his family, but Roger believed that his only health issue was a broken heart due to the loss of his father. Whilst making his way back to his city-centre abode, he flicked the radio on. It was late, but there was always music through the night. 'Make it Easy on Yourself' by the Walker Brothers was playing, one of his dad's favourite songs. A tear fell down his cheek as the bright lights and tall buildings of the former European Capital of Culture came into view. Roger was almost home – in many more ways than one.

EIGHTEEN

Linda had heard no more from Mick, despite having expected him to come over all guns blazing after their phone call on Benny's birthday. She smiled to herself at the idea that he might *just* have seen sense and left her to it. That would suit her just fine. She then tensed her jaw at how she would struggle to get by without his money, which he had given every week, regardless of seeing Benny or not. The last time he had put an envelope through the letterbox, 'for my son' was scrawled upon it in the writing style of someone full of anger.

Linda often enjoyed an argument, the drama of it all: shouting, long-withheld insults being hurled, perhaps a few glasses or plates being smashed. She was quite disappointed that Mick had not turned up. She had planned for if he did – what she would say and do, how she would hurt him with her cutting words. She had even pre-dialed 999 in her phone. If it got nasty she could just press green to call, and the police would come to her aid – just in time to catch what she imagined would be a seething-mad Mick.

Linda was mulling over her intentions from that evening. It would have been unlikely that any police would be able to come to her aid in a hurry should Mick show up at that moment. Her mind had wandered so far, with the help of a bottled friend or three, that she had forgotten what was going on in Merseyside at that moment. Even though local police practically salivated at the mere scent of domestic violence, a killer on the loose would likely be the highlight of their lives and there was no way they were going to miss it: her tall tale would not entice them in the slightest.

Linda's head hurt badly as she went over her thoughts. She was well aware that the amount of alcohol she was imbibing was creeping up each day, and had given thought to addressing it. But as soon as 5 o'clock came, when Benny was home and fed, such thoughts disappeared – and a bottle was opened. She would take numerous paracetamol tablets throughout the day, but nothing could match the hit that the wine gave her: an instant headache cure – until the next day, anyway.

Linda had continued to drink throughout another evening, gazing at programmes which she had no interest in. The yellow alert banner, which had featured on every regional channel the previous evening, was already gone from the main shows and had been relegated back to featuring only on the news channels. Benny had been to school and back without a problem; all schools had been open as normal once again. The boy had eaten his tea and was upstairs in his bedroom on his games console as normal. As Linda sat on the sofa, she began to feel tired – the kind of instant, flick-of-a-switch tiredness that comes with inebriation. She flicked the television off and went to the kitchen as part of her usual efforts to make sure all appliances were switched off prior to going to bed. With heavy eyes, she locked the back door and decided to have a brief sit down at the kitchen table; it was there that her eyelids became all too heavy to keep open, and the table became a makeshift bed.

With her defences down, Linda was not able to see the hate-filled face amidst the darkness, staring at her through the kitchen window. The figure moved towards the back lawn and approached the potted roses. The third one from the left was upturned, as hands sifted hurriedly through the compost with intent and at last found a key encased in a plastic change bag – the emergency key that saved calling an expensive locksmith should the need arise. Returning to the door with haste, Mick slipped the key into the lock with a thief's dexterity – his action was silent. His wrist moved to turn the lock, but it would not budge. He tried again as carefully as he could: he wanted the element of surprise, but *still* the lock would not budge. Linda had ordered them to be changed less than a week after Mick left. It was a move he had not anticipated.

Discretion was ditched, as Mick rattled the key furiously, content that even if he accidentally woke his on-paper-wife he would be able to get to her before she could get to a phone. The rattling became increasingly angered and desperate, causing Linda to stir from her slumber. She eventually raised her head to witness a blurred face through the frosted glass of the back door. It looked truly demonic beneath the moonlight: a squat figure in dark clothing, with a seething red face that could have made a tomato look pale. Linda asked herself if it could be Mick. Before her mind had time to answer, the door was being kicked. It was made of UPVC and had no fewer than three locking points for maximum security from unwanted intruders.

Linda arose from the table, still half-shot from the evening's chardonnay. For one second, she stared at the obscured face of her husband through the glass, remembering the happy times they had once known. That one second proved a timely mistake, as the kicking ceased, and the glass in the top half of the door was shattered by a battered old lump hammer – well-used and with none of the modern ergonomic comforts that modern tools possess: just wood and metal.

Linda fell backwards in fright and saw Mick's arm frantically searching for the key in the other side of the lock as he hurled a relentless tirade of threats and insults her way. To Linda, he looked like a man possessed. Inside, he was. Blood ran down the brilliant-white door. Mick's arm was partially lacerated by the jagged glass that remained. He was past pain at that point. Linda tried to get the key out of the door before he could grab it. As she did so, Mick seized her by her top with a grip like steel on wood.

As he tried to draw her to the glass, she caught a glimpse of his face. It was like nothing she had ever seen before. She had never viewed Mick as a threat. Even when he was angry, he was never aggressive. She knew deep in her heart that she had caused this: she had pushed him too far, but even in her panic, she enjoyed seeing him in such a state. She felt he deserved it. Mick drew her close. The smell of booze filled her nostrils, along with the slightest hint of metal – likely due to the excessive blood loss. She thought that were a match to be struck, Mick may well explode. Mick was bleeding heavily from the glass. She thought that he may have sliced an artery, such was the amount. He had her right next to his face and almost whispered through bared teeth.

"You think you can take everything from me – that I'll just sit down and let you do what you want? You think you can take my son – stop me from seeing my lad?" He tried to draw Linda close to the jagged glass of the door with a strength that was immense and almost impossible to fight against.

"I'll not have him grow up with you poisoning his mind every day – you won't get the chance, you evil bitch: your venom ceases today!" Even in his fury, Mick was surprised at what came out of his mouth. A mild-mannered Scouser, he was not one for grand words. He rarely had all that much to say; at the door in that moment he had sounded almost Shakespearian.

As her throat neared an ominously pointed shard of glass, Linda screamed at the top of her lungs. She put a foot on the door in an effort to pry herself loose of what felt like Lucifer's grip. First it seemed futile, then the cotton strands of her top gave way. She went backwards, with such force that she rolled into the kitchen cupboards. Whilst she was stunned, Mick managed to unlock the door and get into the kitchen.

He came at Linda, still floored, and pounced on top of her like a predator pinning its prey to the ground. He balanced on his knees, straddled above her with the lump-hammer in hand. As he raised it, Linda quickly ascended a bony knee into where it hurt, seized a large stainless steel saucepan from the pan tree on the floor and struck it across Mick's face so hard that it sent him to the floor in a daze. He staggered around on all fours whilst Linda ran to the living room, shutting the solid wood door behind her and barricading it with the nearby sideboard unit. She dug her hands into her pocket for her mobile phone and uttered a repetition of four letter words as she saw the screen had broken, probably due to her fall. The display still functioned, but the inability to use the touchscreen rendered the device useless. She was even more angry that she did not have a house phone: Mick had deemed that there was no point in having one due to the rate of the line rental and the fact that they never used it. She deeply regretted letting him have his way with that one, especially in that very moment.

The door which connected the kitchen and living room started thudding as Mick kicked at it. She had known he would not be stunned long. Each kick brought the sideboard a centimetre further away from the door. She knew it would not be long before he would be through. His shouting got louder, and more manic, by the minute. Linda did not weigh much but tried putting all of her weight behind the sideboard to keep her seemingly-possessed husband out. Her focus was split due to another presence in the room.

"Mum, what's going on?" Benny had come downstairs. How he had slept until now she did not know. In any case, she did not want him to see this. She asked him to stay upstairs. Benny refused to go back to his room, and he started asking her why she was trapping his dad in the kitchen.

"Your dad is a *very* sick man, son. He wants to hurt us, but I won't let him."

Despite the door being solid wood, Mick heard every word of the brief conversation. He completely exploded with anger and began to throw his entire body at the door like a raging bull. The force was such that neither the sideboard nor Linda were effective anymore. He was charging at it, his stocky body acting like a battering ram. He managed enough space to get a hand through, to keep the door wedged and give himself some leverage. Benny looked on in horror as his mum yanked an ornamental candelabra from the wall and began beating his dad's hand with it. Blood soon flowed. There were screams of horror from Benny. There were screams of agony from Mick.

"Mum – stop. Don't hurt him!"

Benny grabbed his mother's arm to stop her striking another blow on his dad's then-mangled hand. Linda turned around. She cracked Benny so hard that he fell over, clutching his face where her nails had caught him. The skin turned to white and then blood began to ebb out. He cried out for his dad to help him. There was nothing that could have fuelled Mick more. With one almighty charge, he burst through with seemingly super-natural force that he sent the sideboard completely over. It landed on Linda's foot: she too fell over as pain surged up her leg. Mick was able to look upon his son. Benny looked back at his dad with a face filled with fear. Mick's left eye had quickly closed and blackened from where the pan had hit him. A scarlet river ran down his head. Blood soiled his clothing from his bicep to his trousers. The glass had sliced through to the artery as he had unlocked the back door. His hand looked like a monstrous claw from where Linda had bashed it repeatedly.

"Dad?"

"Son – are ya alright?" Mick saw blood on Benny's face, running down from scratch marks of his wife's claws. "Did *she* do that to you?

Benny could not get his words out to answer so he nodded timidly.

"You go outside son. Go straight to Frank and Fran's. Ask them to call the police."

The young lad did not question his dad: he was in a state of shock, having never witnessed an event like this before, and obeyed his command without hesitation. As Benny was unlocking the door. Linda began crying out and wailing at the top of her lungs, begging the boy not to go. She told him that his dad would hurt her. Linda did not realise how foolish she had been in her panic: the strike she had dealt Benny had lost her all of his trust in that instant. Benny did as his father asked and sprinted down the driveway, out of the gate and straight down the street.

No words were spoken. Mick scowled at Linda, who had managed to dislodge her foot. She still lay on the ground. The ankle was in a peculiar position. It appeared dislocated. She looked back at Mick with equal hatred:

she knew what was coming. He did not keep her waiting. Two blood-soaked hands flew around her neck and tightened; their grip was was strong and inhuman, more like hydraulic machinery: death by asphyxiation. Linda had never thought about her death – she had thought herself far too young for all that – yet there she lay with a stout, stubby-fingered grim reaper above her.

When the body realises that existence may soon cease, every tiny synapse of the mind is combed in the hope of finding a solution to the impending doom. Even the smallest memory or idea may aid the cause. Linda's mind found just that, as she remembered the novelty sword letter opener that they had bought at a gift shop whilst on holiday in Llandudno. Mick had called it "cheap rubbish," because it was blunt and would not open his letters neatly. He had eventually gone to the trouble of sharpening its edges. Linda had never bothered using the item – it was more ornamental than anything – but her mind had remembered where it was kept. Whilst her vision began to blacken and fade, as her bronchioles pleaded to be filled with air once again, she somehow searched with her right arm along the sideboard. She felt the top draw handle and tugged with what dwindling strength remained in her. The draw itself hung open, courtesy of gravity. Mick was focused solely on his wife's dying face. He had wanted to kill her before he got to the house. He might not have gone through with it, but striking Benny had sealed her fate. In his mind, and with the amount of force he was putting into his hands, he knew that his goal – her end – was most definitely near.

Mick's hands suddenly lost their strength and instantly flew from his wife's neck to his own. Linda gasped out as her body tried to refuel, making up for the near fatal loss of oxygen it had just endured. She had thrust the letter opener directly into Mick's neck. Blood was spurting out in small intermittent streams similar to the squirts of a child's water pistol. Mick lay on the floor, also gasping. He yanked out the letter opener and tried to seal the gap with his palm. He rolled over and tried to get back on his feet, but he only managed to get to his knees. His fingers proved to be a poor dam for the red river beckoning behind them.

Linda saw his weakened state and managed to get up herself, giving him a strong kick in the gut with her good foot. The other one was still in an unnatural position and hurting from the sideboard having fallen upon it. Mick rolled and crawled for the sofa, desperate for anything that he could use to raise himself to his feet again. He was too prone to assault whilst on all fours. Linda was amazed at the speed at which her husband could still move. His injuries and the amount of blood now decorating the floor made it hard to imagine that there was any more than a few drops left in his damaged body. Mick disappeared into the kitchen. Linda feared he was making an escape.

Police sirens could be heard in the distance, drawing nearer. She knew that Benny must have made it to Frank and Fran's place. She was still fearful of Mick, but she knew that he would not stand a chance against the police in the state that he was in. She also knew that he would not get far. If he left, the police would catch him in no time – though she was not prepared to take the chance of him getting away, however slight it might be. Linda wanted Mick to be arrested. She wanted him to go to jail. She wanted him to suffer. Youth was not on his side, he was small and he would be an ideal target for those looking to make a big noise and build a hardman reputation in prison. On that thought, she chased after him into the kitchen where the once immaculate tiled floor was now awash with both blood and glass.

Mick was leaning on the kitchen table with one hand. The was other around his neck, trying to stem the blood flow. Linda had not realised that he could see her reflection in the chrome extractor fan. He watched as she lifted a knife from the counter. He watched as she came at him. He wheeled around with the lump hammer. Fortunately for Linda, the carving knife was lighter, longer and had greater reach. She had used it earlier to cut up some watermelon for Benny – it was supposed to be used for slicing large joints of meat, but her poor choice of utensil had turned out to be a most vital choice in the end. The knife went into Mick's stomach with minimal effort. The hammer instantly dropped from his hand to the floor; it may have broken a tile or two, but there was so much blood that it was impossible to tell. She took one look into his pitiful eyes. Still her hatred for him remained. She was not about to give mercy. Instead, she twisted the knife. Her husband cried out in agony and fell to the floor as a searing pain raged through him.

Linda made her way back to the front of the house.

The front door was still wide open from when Benny had left. The boy had not looked back as he had fled. The darkness of the living room was filled with flashes of blue. The entire avenue looked to be flooded with police cars and armed-response vans. Linda put an arm to shield her face from the blinding spotlight aimed at her. A voice came through a megaphone, though even the distortion could not disguise the local accent of the voice at the other end.

"Stop where you are and do exactly as I say! Put your hands above your head and drop to your knees – slowly! We are armed and *will* fire if necessary. Do you understand?"

Linda was shocked at just how volatile the situation was. She had imagined the police coming to her aid straight away, bursting into the house to whisk her out whilst slapping handcuffs on Mick and hauling him away. She stood in a daze not knowing what to do or say – her mind had temporarily relinquished its command of the body in which it was encased.

"I repeat. Put your hands above your head and drop to your knees! We *are* armed and we *will* shoot if you do not comply! Do you understand?"

As her eyes adjusted to what felt like a solar flare from the spotlights in the dark abyss of a ghastly evening, Linda saw that there were several armed police with guns aimed at her. She could not believe it: she did not understand why she was being aimed at. She had only seen situations like this on the television: the victim was never under any threat. In her mind she had always been the victim – she never accepted blame for problems, even if she had blatantly caused them herself. Linda tried to speak but her mouth could not move properly to pronounce the words. The megaphone began to bark at her yet again when a tremendous force hit her from behind and sent her to the floor on the path of her front garden.

Linda heard the sound of chaotic charging as the armed and armoured police moved in. It was the not her sense of hearing that left her petrified in that moment – it was her sense of sight. Mick had made one final charge, one last blast of the trumpet on a battlefield upon which he was destined for defeat. The numerous police marksmen had not caught sight of him because of where Linda had been stood in the doorway. If she had just done what the police had asked, he would have been dealt with. Instead, he was atop her again, hammer in hand, aiming for her face. His blows, though now laboured, were still powerful enough to kill her should he hit his target – a goal he was to be denied due to a combination of his wife's writhing and his laboured movement due to his injuries.

He had *one* good swing that would have hit her square in the face – but Linda just got her head out of the way in time and the blow hit her shoulder instead, right on the collarbone. The pain was excruciating and she fought to get her husband off of her, but he was too heavy. All she could do was roll – preventing him from balancing and making an accurate attack. There was screaming from the police; it was completely incoherent given the situation. The rolling was preventing Mick from gaining much strength behind his attempted swipes and also preventing police from getting a clear shot. Linda felt the cold steel graze her face several times, missing her by less than an inch. She tried to claw back at Mick's face and managed to get a hand to it. She pulled it away instantly when Mick let out an agonising groan, what she felt with her fingertips left her nauseated. The strike with the pan earlier must have shattered his eye socket because the moment she touched that injured part of his face, the eye fell out and dangled on its optic stalk.

The rolling stopped, as Mick put everything he had into pinning his wife down using his full weight– a mass which she could not even hope to budge. Mick raised the hammer high one final time as Linda put her hands in front of her face in a pitiful attempt at defence. She knew the next blow *would* finish her.

Mick's body shook as though he was attempting some bizarre robotic dance move. The sound of gunfire, which had rented the silent air, ceased after mere seconds. Linda lay in total shock as her husband's bloodied and decimated body slumped lifelessly onto her. She tried to focus and make sense of what had just happened. It did not feel like reality to her, she was waiting to wake up any second but inside she knew it was all too real to be false. Despite all the horror of that had occurred that night – despite the fact that she lay beneath the still-warm corpse of her husband, Linda felt a certain pride within herself as she realised Mick would not be getting back up again. Mick's last stand was finished: Linda had won. Mick's dead and grotesquely damaged face lay right against hers and – before the police had a chance to come and remove the body – she smiled at it. She looked forward to the comfortable life that lay ahead, freed from the millstone that was once her husband.

NINETEEN

Another cloud-filled sky engulfed Liverpool, giving the day a grey hue like an old, faded photograph. Born and bred in Merseyside, Roger always enjoyed looking out across the city. Back when he was a boy, he had loved visiting the Anglican cathedral, just so he could go and stare at the sights from the top of it. He had been a Catholic back then, which was an ironic coincidence. Lately, Roger did not know what he believed in anymore. He had considered going to confession but thought better of it – just in case his plan was foiled before he completed it. The pivotal piece of the jigsaw needed to be in place, lest it remain incomplete and have all been for nothing. Though the confession was essentially to God through the medium of a priest, Roger did not want to test the limits of the Seal of Confession and risk one of God's servants running to the police. Instead, Roger went to the smaller church at the top of Prescot Street, told the priest that he was terminally ill and asked for the last rites sacrament. The priest asked him what his condition was.

"Terminal." Roger replied briefly in an effort to avoid further interrogation. His lie was believed because he did not look at all like a well man. He had gone very thin from a poor diet where he had completely forgotten to eat some days and just drank instead – self medication. The booze was taking its toll and had given Roger a ruddy complexion. The stress of being a judge had almost doubled his wrinkles on his face and the grey hairs on his head, which had been jet black not so long ago in the grand scheme of time. The priest gave him the sacrament for the 'anointing of the sick' – which had become the modern day term for 'last rites.' Roger accepted this and just decided that something was better than nothing: *'once a Catholic, always a Catholic,' they say.*

Roger had to keep up with the news: he was a judge, and current affairs were a priority – especially when they involved him. He did a lot of research into his cases: he had been studying what was to be his final case since he first set out to ensure that the guilty went punished. So much justice had been carried out during his time in the role, and the final court case was soon to take place.

He had saved the most important until last, the one he most desired to bring his gavel down upon, one who truly deserved to face the hammer of justice. He had been watching Linda Painter for some weeks. He had noted the lack of her husband's presence at the house and had been on the verge of presenting her with her summons. He envisaged that he would still be the star of the show, though he craved no credit for his actions, he only wanted for people recognise that those who were sentenced were not fit to walk the earth. *If dad isn't here, then why should they be?*

He put the news on one evening to see a major story breaking. Roger was amazed to see that another attraction had taken centre stage – an attraction which involved the *very person* who *he* had been tracking and was soon due for *their* day in court. This would have been a major setback were it not for a sizeable slice of good fortune: the husband had attacked her and the journalists were already making their minds up that *he* was the so-called Neo Ripper. Even the police were suggesting as much but, as usual, they were delaying the release of an official statement.

Roger had little time for clichés, but dead men told no tales, and with at least five bullets in him, the husband would certainly not be denying that he was responsible for the countrywide murders. Roger did not know much about Michael Painter; he had been no concern of his, since he had not been living at the house for several months. He knew Linda's movements though: she was very predictable, mainly going out for shopping or to take her boy to school. Michael would serve as a martyr to Roger's cause, and if anything, he was glad Michael had not succeeded in killing his spouse. Roger wanted her to face the criminal justice he would personally deliver to her.

After all the sentences Roger had passed, Linda's was to be the most important of the lot. She had been the cold and calculated machine that started it all, by wielding her powers against a man who had paid his dues throughout his life and ended up in need of a little help. Roger had often noted that some of the people on Disability Living Allowance were *far* from disabled, and so many of them were so young. This had led him to believe that his dad would have no problem getting it. He had heard from numerous friends that almost everyone gets turned down on their first assessment, but it is the second that is most important: the senior assessor's decision carried a lot more clout. It had been horrible watching his dad sit there and be questioned by some rodent-esque 'bint' who had not liked Billy Birch from the moment he stepped through the door.

Roger had done a lot of research at the time and spoken to a lot of people. The government were still adamant that too many people were on DLA, and the Yankee organisation that they had running the operation were given strict assessment criteria to follow and figures to meet. It was impossible to find out what they were, but it was similar to a driving test – when a hopeful learner pulls up outside the test centre and has already failed before they are seen because too many people have already passed that day. They become a victim of figures. Nobody ever truly knows such things other than the assessors, who keep it all under lock and key. Roger was convinced that was the case with his dad on the day of that assessment. He had stared piercingly into the eyes of *that* so-called senior assessor towards the end. Her facial expression had not changed, but her eyes had: the eyes gave it all away. She was uncomfortable and perhaps a little intimidated. Her hand had also switched position, and Roger would not be surprised if there had been a security button beneath the desk. It was ultimately her fault that the death of his father came so quickly: she was the catalyst. Roger had spent countless hours thinking about it all.

It could be argued that the doctor missing the cancer was the prime cause, but even then, his dad would have had some time to live: time him and Roger could have enjoyed together, making the most of life. The job situation had crippled Billy internally: his confidence was gone. Had he been thinking like his usual self, he would never have fallen for the trap set by the fraudster. All the while, Billy was trying his best to survive on part-time hours in a completely alien work environment, where he was bullied by a supervisor half his age, and forced to breaking point. An arrest by the police had proved all too much, and his heart had gone on the doorstep. The ambulance crew had tried to get it to beat again, but in truth, it had not beaten for a long time. Billy had ended up just a walking shell of a man, and was living each day content in the knowledge that if the good lord told him it was time, he would neither grumble nor argue.

The rotten foundation on which this entire house of horrors was built was Linda Painter, and Roger was adamant that she above all others was going to face justice: *divine justice indeed.* He had promised his dad on his deathbed that he would avenge him, and a promise in such circumstances is not one that can be broken – no matter how rash it may seem in hindsight. *Beds are made and must be lain in, regardless.*

All of the pillars had been put in place for one final ceremony on the morbid altar that Roger had found himself on. He had questioned his own actions many a time, and his mind always found a way of reminding him that his victims deserved the punishment that they received.

Karma, comeuppance – whatever fancy new name they gave it in the modern era, he knew he was in the right, and once he got fired up, he could not stop until the entirety of the fuel in the furnace was exhausted. Roger sat amidst the tip that was his apartment. It looked like it had been burgled, with items strewn everywhere. It had been tidy once, but as retirement grew closer, Roger cared less for minor things such as household order. Order in the courtroom took priority. Many was the time he would fling things around, breaking his personal possessions. To a fly on the wall, it may have seemed futile; to Roger, it was therapy. When things became too much, and when his blood-alcohol level increased, shattering what was his old, meticulous order helped alleviate the pressure.

As the news revealed further information, Roger sat with the armchair facing the window, looking across the city, down the banks of the Mersey, past the docks and towards Crosby. He was always more one for listening to the news than watching it: a different generation. A hot, almost sickening sensation hit him out of the blue, as his body tried to remind him that it had more than a sufficient level of whiskey within it. Roger's mind knew differently though: he needed it. He sought inebriation: it was the only way that he could achieve a temporary ceasefire in the war zone that was his mind. The final court case was almost upon him, but he knew he must wait until the media attention died down a little. *Two weeks, max – it always is with the news.* The bottle tilted upwards once again, as Roger's head tilted backwards to swallow the potent liquid; as it came down, the broken man that was Roger Birch cried out in anguish.

"Oh dad!" He burst into a series of sobs, both from the thoughts about his father, and the fact that this saga was almost at an end. One last court case and it would all be done, whether he joined his father in heaven or not: at least he had done right by him. Recomposing himself, and managing to stand up, Roger leaned on the panoramic window with one hand and kept hold of his bottle with the other. He began to fixate on Crosby again which caused his eyes to narrow and his teeth to grind hard together. The catalyst was soon to face justice – *and bloody hell, will she face justice indeed.*

TWENTY

It had been a rollercoaster of a few days for Linda. When she had woken up on that fateful morning, she had never expected the day would end with her husband being gunned down by police marksmen before her. In truth, she had never even expected that he would come after her in the manner that he had. She *had* thought that she knew Mick inside out, but clearly he had a few surprises hiding in the back of his mind. She had spent the night in the accident and emergency department of Aintree Hospital, whilst her injuries were treated. The ankle had turned out to be dislocated and was easily righted, whilst the rest of her injuries were just cuts and heavy bruising.

Whilst at the hospital, she had been accompanied by a police officer. She was surprised when others arrived and asked her question after question about Mick's other activities, what she knew of him and where she thought he may have been recently. There were just so many questions – too many. It felt more like an interrogation, a feeling which was amplified when she was discharged from the hospital and taken to Copy Lane Police Station. She was still in shock, and her mind had not seemed to process the blindingly obvious fact that the police believed that her husband was the Neo Ripper.

All she had wanted to do was get back to her son. He had been left in the care of Frank and Frances. Forensic data needed to be collected from her house, and a police station was no place for a young boy to spend his day. It had hurt Linda greatly when a female officer told her that she would have to wait to see her son. Linda had protested so much that the officer was forced to stop sugar-coating the issue and tell her that Benny had insisted that he did not want to see his mother. Linda hated that Mick had made that happen: it was all his fault. Worse still, she had struck her son. Police had informed her that the incident would need to be investigated further. She had already been questioned about it, and deeply regretted not requesting a lawyer. She had thought that they would be making a fuss of her and checking that she was okay – not treating her like a criminal when she was the *victim*.

The police had put Linda up in a hotel for several nights whilst her property was thoroughly searched. It had seemed like a nice gesture at first, but she soon realised that she was very much a prisoner and that the room was more of a cell than a refuge. The door was guarded by a uniformed officer. Part of the reason for her sentinel had been because of the manic press that would be hounding her if they knew where she was, desperate for photographs and salivating at the prospect of a quote – the other part was that the police believed Linda knew more about the killings than she had divulged in interviews and may well have aided her husband in them. Days passed, and countless trips were made between the station and hotel. Literally hundreds of questions were asked by different officers, doctors, counsellors and inspectors – until Linda was finally released and permitted to return home.

Previously, Linda had only seen crime scenes on the television, and she had been under the impression that the house would be nicely prepared for her return, made to look as though nothing had happened. The reality was that it was worse than when she had last seen it: as she was wheeled away on a gurney – an act completed prior to Mick being zipped up in a body bag. The forensics team had well and truly turned the place upside down in their search. It felt so empty without Benny, but it would take a long time before he would be able to return home. That was if he would even want to – and if she would even be *allowed* to look after him again.

Linda made a start to the cleanup operation by picking up some large pieces of smashed glass in the kitchen – it seemed a futile effort given the nature of the destruction, but she had to start somewhere. After a few trips to the bin, she made her way to the fridge and remembered that the wine she had opened should still be there. A smile beamed across her face as her assumption was correct. She paused for a moment as she looked across at the back door, where Mick had made his final entrance. She was amazed at how she could smile, but she continued to do so nevertheless. The door had been covered by a large metal plate to prevent break-ins; it was the same type that the council used to seal up empty houses in rough areas.

Linda had hated Mick for some months, and the fact that he was now dead made no difference to how she felt. She had loved him once, but that was well in the past, and she even questioned whether that feeling could have been merely lust. One of the counsellors who Linda saw at the police station had explained the stages of grief with her briefly, but Linda had little time for all of that: she always knew better and was of firm belief that the only person who truly understood her was herself. It was on that thought that the idea finally hit her that Mick may have been the Neo Ripper. She began going through all of the killings she had remembered hearing about on the news and questioned whether Mick would have been capable of them – as well as what motive he would have had to undertake such gruesome acts. Sometimes, if it stumbles upon something new, the mind can latch onto it and convince all old thoughts to jump ship. This was exactly what was happening to Linda. The fact that he had come to kill her had illustrated to her most clearly that she did not truly know her late husband. Little did she realise that Mick's last stand was borne solely from her own actions.

Linda carried on tidying up whilst making sure to stay topped up on chardonnay. There were several rings of the doorbell, and the phone went a few times: journalists. Even though she was ex-directory, no information is truly hidden in the digital age. She saw several people pass the house, throughout the course of the day, trying to have a look in. A few inadvertently identified themselves as journalists as they clumsily tried, and failed, to get a photo without making their actions obvious. One man did just pull out his camera and even began to walk like a crab, sidestepping in the way that some photographers do in order to get a better shot. Linda was disgusted at the gall of him, but in a weird kind of way she loved the attention she was getting. There was one strange man who caught her eye as she drifted from room to room. Tall, dark-haired and wearing a black jacket. He did not look like a journalist, but she did not recognise him as a neighbour. She presumed he must be a ghoul from afar who had come to see the famous Crosby murder house, as she was sure it would one day be referred to in books and documentaries.

All that Linda was truly concerned about was getting her son back and regaining order in her life. She had already been considering seeing if there were any jobs at the government offices still available, but she knew from those with whom she had kept in touch that the job market was very different to how it was when she left. It would be hard to tell Benny exactly what had happened, but it would probably be someone else who would tell him first, as she knew she would not be seeing him until social services sanctioned it. Schools can be cruel places: many parents fill their children's minds with their own prejudices, and she dreaded what Benny may be going through. On that thought, the red mist descended upon her mind again: if the boy had not seen her attack Mick, it would have been okay: he would be there with her now. Her blood boiled beneath the skin, and she finished the almost-full glass of wine in one quick gulp, as she cursed Mick for what he had caused.

It was a desolate existence Linda was living, but as

each day went by, the crowd of photographers on the street grew fewer and fewer; after about a fortnight, it was only a few very young boys in tight-fitting trousers carrying notepads and small cheap cameras that were hanging carelessly around their necks. They were either on work experience placements or were newsroom newbies. The papers had given up wasting their highest-paid journalists on a story people were already tired of hearing about, such was the news. The young ones were generally too nervous to ask anything in the intimidating way of their seasoned higher-ups, and Linda was soon able to relax and go back and forth to the shops in peace.

Happiness was beyond her, as her mind was completely consumed with rage towards Mick. A series of DNA tests were being carried out, and it was proving a lengthy post mortem. She had intended to urinate on his grave – one final cutting insult which he would be able to do nothing about – until she remembered he preferred cremation. She would have forced a burial, but she knew that he had written his preferences in his last will and testament, which he had made shortly after Benny was born. Plot foiled, she made the decision in her head that she would flush his ashes down the toilet the moment that she received them. Nobody was going to have the last laugh on Linda Painter.

TWENTY ONE

Roger had passed the house of his defendant several times over the course of a fortnight. He had watched the number of people outside die down, like flies eventually growing tired of a hardening dog turd. Journalists and plain-clothes police officers had surrounded the place; now there were just one or two spotty young reporters, who spent most of their time on their mobile phones and left promptly at 5pm. It was time for the final hearing: the catalyst was to face the hammer of justice.

It had been a cloudy, drizzly, April day in Liverpool. The weather had worsened gradually until the light rain predicted for the afternoon turned into the heavy rain which had been anticipated for the evening. Roger had passed the house once more, just for one final stakeout to see if there was anything else that he needed to take into consideration. He always liked to be certain of things and such an event as this held no room for careless errors.

The almost-retired judge had navigated the promenade and sands of Crosby several times throughout the day, Anthony Gormley's Iron Men being the exact type of company he craved. He could say what he wanted to them, tell them his plans in detail and talk of the anguish he had gone through – and was still suffering from. The corroded, humanoid figures stared their rusty gaze his way, neither arguing nor ignoring any of the important information which he was conveying.

Roger had done his best to maintain sobriety, but the tremors resonating from deep within his body had become too much. He found himself reaching for his coat pocket. The bottle had been brought along for his retirement party: it was supposed to be saved for celebration; out of necessity, it was opened early. Not much was consumed though – despite having descended into somewhat of an alcoholic, Roger was what is described in many an AA meeting as a 'functioning alcoholic': he was still able to go about his daily tasks. These tasks were not the typical actions of an average person in a normal life; Roger was adamant that they needed doing nevertheless. Surveillance, study, planning and, at times, prayer – they were all part of his routine. Roger had prayed a lot that final day: to his dad, to his mum – there were even some to God, who he did not quite believe would welcome him with open arms but – he hoped – would understand why he had done what he did over the past year or so.

On his final circuit of the beach, Roger made his way for one last coffee at his favourite snack and beverage van. He hoped it would be there, and to his delight, it was indeed there – despite the bad weather. The owner was in the process of closing up, and Roger was grateful to have just caught it: he was a man of ritual and needed things to go according to plan – on that day, more than he ever had in his life. Roger felt like it was almost a sign from the good lord, as though he was giving Roger the go-ahead: normally on rainy days, it was never there; sometimes it did not even show up on sunny days. He ordered a hot chocolate with cream and marshmallows, as well as a big slice of home-made cake.

The order may have seemed like that of a child's selection, but Roger had always found it amusing: humanity worshipped alcohol, yet social convention dictated that a love of sweet foods and treats was reserved for solely for children. Any attempt to indulge in such pleasure diluted a man's masculinity. The look that the woman gave him as he placed his order only backed up his views on that matter, but he was not about to be denied one small pleasure on what was likely to be his last day on the planet. He was long past caring what people thought of him anyway.

The afternoon was cold, wet and windy, so he enjoyed every last sip of his fancy beverage all the more. Some of the cake blew away, but the resident starlings made short work of it. Diversions had been enjoyed, and it was time to get down to business. The sun was setting over the River Mersey, turning the sky an initial picturesque pink before a foreboding crimson. The house he was to invade was only a short walk up from the shore.

Darkness was taking a firm grip upon what was left of the daylight. He would soon present the immediate summons. The shakes had returned to Roger on the way to the house; he was surprised at how quickly they had come back: he blamed them on the hot chocolate diluting the potency of the alcohol in his system. Normally a stiff drink would abate his tremors, but he was still shaking after another hearty slug straight from the bottle. He put it down to nerves and forced himself to carry on walking until he was almost outside the house. The nearby Crosby Village shopping centre had entered the newspaper on many an occasion for its awful parking facilities, but just a few minutes up the road on Acacia Avenue there were countless spaces available to park on the street. Roger had laughed to himself at how blatantly he was able to park his van in front of an unoccupied house with an overgrown garden; the residents of the neighbourhood were so busy getting home improvements done and trying to outdo one-another that a strange vehicle raised no eyebrows.

Darkness had completely swallowed up what daylight there was left in the sky. Roger's choice of black clothing provided substantial camouflage. The moon and stars were hidden by the clouds, and the energy-efficient streetlights kept the avenue as black as coal, lighting only for brief periods when cars passed. He had tampered with the wiring of the three nearest to Linda's house during the early hours of that morning in preparation. None of the previous cases had made the judge so nervous, but this climactic one was an intricately-planned event, which he was desperate to get right.

He strode to the pavement opposite her driveway and saw the living room light on. The curtains were closed, but the lack of inner lining made it easy to make out a silhouette through them. He watched the figure move. What some may call tall and slender, Roger described as gaunt and scrawny: he liked a 'proper' woman with round hips and a 'decent chest' and, to him, this 'business bitch' was a living parody of everything that was wrong with the modern day ideal woman.

Though he was unable to see her properly at that moment, he remembered the 'sow' had worn a grey trouser-suit on the day she icily denied his father that which he should have been entitled to. Rage, venom and pain filled the judge's heart as a tremendous discomfort surged through his left arm. He had many sore muscles of late; collapsing into a drunken sleep on his floor on a regular basis had not helped matters, and he put this pain down to booze too. A quick check of the street: it was both empty and silent except for a dog barking intermittently in the distance. This was it: judgement day had arrived.

Roger went to the back of his van and grabbed his toolbox: *tools of the trade.* He made his way up the driveway, carefully opening and closing the gate without so much as a sound, and proceeded to the back garden. The door was still sealed shut with a metal plate, and all of the windows were the double-glazed high-security style – almost impenetrable. Roger began to become frustrated as he ran his hands along them, searching for a gap or anything that he could slide a tool down. Nothing.

There were windows upstairs, but accessing them would be difficult. This was partly due to being the wrong side of 40 and partly due to the fact that he had never been very agile in the first place. He did not fancy failing his mission due to some ridiculous fall. He gritted his teeth in fury as he strained his mind, trying to think up a backup plan. The initial idea he had was to follow Linda home, but he liked the idea of darkness. He wanted her to be truly terrified, and no nightmare creature ever reared its head in broad daylight – nor even dusk: it had to be pitch black for maximum impact. The judge had planned for this day for more than a year; the court date could not be set back. He was a man of routine, and everything had been put in place: last rites given, a will made out to animal charities and a letter sent to local papers first class. The last one was the most crucial, and it would be a matter of hours until it was received – if Royal Mail did their job properly. It could not be unsent, and if Roger did not do what was required of him that night, then his entire campaign would have been for nothing.

Just as panic started to set in, his mind came to a ridiculously simple conclusion. He paced carefully back to the front porch and placed a hand on the front door handle. Pushing with such little force that it would barely register on a Newton-meter, Roger made the handle descend with a barely-audible click from the mechanism. He marvelled at how careless someone could be to leave the door unlocked – especially after enduring an ordeal of the type Linda had. He lifted his toolbox and entered the dark hallway as quietly as he could, ensuring he made no sounds to accompany the chuntering television and of the fridge excommunicating whatever heat had tried to invade it. Small strips of light leaked out from the bottoms of the doors in the hallway – the one which led to the living room had a shadow splitting it in two, which indicated to Roger that the harpy was behind door number one. He closed the front door as quietly as he had opened it and, with the same silent precision, he engaged its locks. Linda may have taken her personal security lightly, but Judge Birch was not about to have any runaways in his courtroom. Gripping the rounded brass knob and twisting his wrist anticlockwise, Roger proceeded to open the door with considerable force. He was ready to bring an end to his nightmare, *divine closure.*

TWENTY TWO

The room was empty. Roger's eyes darted at an alarming speed, like a crazed housefly that has just inhaled a generous gulp of insecticide. There was no sight of Linda, but the door to the kitchen was ajar. He had ridden his luck like a racehorse and was hoping to God that he would make it over the final hurdle.

He walked towards the kitchen without making a sound, a feat that was made even easier with the deep-pile living room carpet beneath him. There was evidence of a previous scuffle – the one the television had told him about. The kitchen door looked badly damaged, as did the walls around it. The carpet too was in dire need of a clean: blood had stained it and was yet to be scrubbed out. The court case would ensure that Roger added to it: he intended imposing a sentence most harsh.

The judge peered through the gap in the door and there she was: the defendant, filling herself full of wine. She sat with a bottle on the table and an empty glass. It was a white wine. Leaving it out of the fridge was an act seldom practised by anyone other than drinkers who intended to consume the lot, glass after glass. Linda had just finished a glass and shook the bottle, peering at it in a questioning manner. She rose from her seat. Roger gazed on at the 'mousey bitch' who had ruined at least two lives with her harsh actions. He was not bothered about

144

his own life any more, but he did sometimes wonder what might have been had everything not been shattered by the untimely – and so very unnecessary – death of his father. The moment felt surreal. He had judged so many, took so many risks, yet somehow managed to get to where he was at that moment: about to complete his quest.

His loss of focus, in that brief moment of thought, was brought to an abrupt halt: he saw Linda coming towards the door. He panicked for a moment. His chest tightened – he reckoned it was due to the fact that his body sensed that there was booze nearby. Linda did not return to the living room. Instead, she opened a drawer and fidgeted with her hands, before putting them to her mouth: *tablet*. She then proceeded to the fridge. The judge could wait no more. The time he had spent peering through the door, at the witch-like figure of the being he loathed more than any other, had made his blood run stone cold. He could withstand the hatred no longer: he had to give in to it. At long last, he had the opportunity to do so. Had the door creaked, the all-important element of surprise would have been lost. Fortune favoured the judge. In less than five strides, he was behind his defendant. The moment was euphoric for Roger – but at the same time, it was sickening to be so close to the one he despised.

Linda was tipsy – but not drunk enough to inhibit the sixth-sense feeling of a presence looming behind her – *a large, ominous presence*. In that split second, she gazed at the white sheen of the fridge. There was indeed a figure behind her. She wheeled around to look, convinced it was Mick – though this figure was more than a foot taller and alive. There stood a man, tall and dark-haired, dressed completely in black. He was in need of a shave. His nose and face, both red, made him look very unwell. He seemed familiar; she was unable to recall just where she had seen his face before.

The short epoch in time that she had to gaze upon him expired rapidly, as did the oxygen in her body: a meaty hand had wrapped itself around her neck as fast as lightening. No words were spoken. The figure had his teeth bared. He drew his face close to hers, glaring at her with a repulsed and reviled expression. Linda tried to struggle, but the man was strong – stronger than Mick had been. A kick to his fragile area was attempted, but he saw it coming and dodged the assault easily. He counterattacked, slamming her against the fridge and restricting her airway further with an even tighter grip. Her head bounced off the unit, and the impact rattled her brains.

"Do you know who I am?" The judge questioned the defendant. Dazed, afraid and struggling to breathe, she tried to make an effort to recognise the hate-filled face before her. Linda's mind scanned and searched through her memories, but she was too slow for the judge's liking. He slammed her against the fridge again. Her legs went limp. The arm, which was pinning her in position, was more than strong enough to hold her up. Roger was a big man, but no bodybuilder: his strength in that moment was borne from anger.

"Look at me! Who am I? Tell me *who* I am!" Her

attacker's voice was deafening. He was an inch or so away from her face. She would have found the smell of whiskey on his breath overpowering, but having had a skinful of wine herself made it barely noticeable. Linda's eyes began to roll as she started to feel her consciousness fade. Just as it did, her mind found a pivotal memory – like the needle on an old hard drive finally locating a file. The hand relinquished its grip. Her body collapsed to the floor like a sack of potatoes. The judge was not seeking a quick trial.

Roger proceeded back to the hall to retrieve his tool-box. As he bent down to pick it up, a flash of pain went through his skull. Linda had hit him over the head with a wooden rolling pin – a bizarre choice of weapon: she had opened the bottom drawer when getting back up, and that had been the first item to hand that could function as a weapon. Roger was furious with himself. He had enough experience, from his court cases, to know that people did not stay knocked-out in real life as long as they did in the movies. Still, he had thought a few minutes was a general rule of thumb.

Linda fumbled desperately at the door. The handle would not budge. She looked for where the key should be. Roger had already covered that escape route. As she went to flee the hallway, he grabbed one of her legs. She fell to the ground in an attempt to run. She tried to kick at her floored aggressor, but he fought off the kicks with one hand whilst feeling in the dark for his hammer. The pair both got to one knee at the same time. Linda was slightly younger and more able-bodied, but Roger was older and had gained plenty of combat experience during his time on the planet.

His right hand had grasped a wooden handle. His left hand pulled back the left leg of the defendant. He brought down his hammer of justice before having even asked his defendant a proper question. A loud crunch resounded – a sound that may not have seemed too out of place during crab night at a seafood restaurant. It even sickened Roger slightly: he had not expected a direct connection with the knee. Linda wailed like a banshee. The judge got back to his feet. His head throbbed, and he felt nauseous. He picked up the toolbox – successfully this time – and with his other hand, he grabbed the tightly-wrapped bun that was the hair of his defendant. He dragged her to the kitchen, where he had decided that the hearing would take place. He threw her into one of the dining chairs and bound her hands with some old, rough rope he had pulled from his toolbox. It felt like burning upon her skin. He tied it extra tight, securing her arms to the dining chair. Roger would usually secure defendants feet as well. The hammer blow had rendered that unnecessary.

Linda's left leg throbbed with pain. She switched frantically between feeling like passing out and wanting to vomit. Her right ankle still ached, following the dislocation during her scuffle with Mick. Linda had not feared Mick, despite the fact that he tried to kill her. There was something about Roger which put the fear of God into her. She tried to speak to him without puking – it was more difficult than she imagined.

"P– please… I think I remember you now."

Roger had started to take a gulp of the whiskey he had left in the bottle earlier; he instantly stopped as Linda spoke.

"So who am I then?" He asked the question in an almost reasonable tone. Linda saw it as a glimmer of hope.

"Y-you, you were with an old man – your dad, I think."

"And do you remember what *you* did?"

Again, he spoke in an eerily calm tone. Linda could not remember the action she took. She knew that she must have turned him down for something. What she did remember clearly were the eyes. The eyes that now glared at her were the same eyes that had glared at her in her office. The man had said nothing as he sat behind his dad during the assessment meeting. At the time, she had thought him cowardly, but now she thought that he had been planning this day from that very moment. The truth was, he had not. It was only *after* Billy Birch died that Roger went the way he did. There had been other wrongdoings along the way. He had never taken action previously, whilst his dad was still alive, but the unjust death of a loved one can have a tremendous impact upon the mind.

"I *think* I turned him down for a benefit…"

"**YOU THINK? YOU THIIIINK?**" Roger's voice boomed. Whatever tranquillity and composure there had been to it had expired."You destroyed that man's life: my father – me dad – me best mate. You killed him!"

For one moment, Linda lost her fear. Perhaps it was

the old office attitude having been awoken again. She replied curtly, as though she was not tied in a chair with a shattered knee, sat before a crazed giant of a man with a toolbox.

"And how, exactly, could *I* have done that?"

Roger cracked her across the face, closed-fisted. The taste of blood flooded her mouth, and an incisor hung loosely from a ribbon of red flesh, not loose enough to be detached completely.

"You're on trial here, love. I ask the questions and you will learn of your actions – and I guarantee you will answer for them – *oh you will indeed!*"

Roger proceeded to go through his father's story, ensuring to specify in every instance how it all boiled down to Linda. When she tried to argue, he struck her again and again. She tried several times, until the pain became too much, and she just sat there and listened to what she considered the ravings of a lunatic. Linda had no sympathy for his father or the man standing before her. She would gladly kill them both now if it meant that she could escape the predicament she was in; she would gladly watch them both suffer. As Roger went on, she began to switch off – partly from pain, partly from a lack of interest. As soon as Roger clocked on, she instantly felt an iron grip around her almost-fleshless forearm – and then total agony as actual iron came down and sandwiched her carpus between metal and solid wood. Linda yelled out in a deafening scream of agony, but Roger bellowed over her.

"I *will* have order in my courtroom. You're on trial

and you *will* listen to what I have to say!"

Roger went to continue his speech, but Linda began relentlessly screaming. He did not know whether it was to try and attract attention or to drown him out, but it infuriated the judge. He had to maintain order. He struck her. The din ceased for a moment, then began again. Stronger measures were required. He rummaged frantically through his toolbox, until he found the particular instrument he was looking for. Linda continued to scream like a banshee, until her jawbone was seized. The sound of 100 blackboards being scraped seared through her skull, as metal pliers closed around one of her front teeth – a horrible feeling. She tried to apologise and beg Roger to stop. He stared down at her, but she could not get her words out due to the tool residing in her mouth. The judge tightened his grip further and yanked the tooth out. He was no dentist. There was no fluidity to his actions. Linda thought that she would pass out from the pain, but fate denied her such good fortune as she endured it all, fully conscious. Roger brandished the tooth in front of her, like a turd to a puppy that had just defecated indoors. The coppery nerve ending hung out like an electrical wire.

"You will listen. If you refuse, I'll take another every time you open that stupid gob of yours."

Linda sobbed as the gaping hole bled heavily and a warm flow ran down her chin.

"I'd take your tongue, but I'll be wanting a confession."

Roger continued letting her know in as much detail

as possible how her selfish actions had brought about the demise of his dad. He told her how he had studied her job, how it worked, and what targets she had – and the bonuses received for meeting them. He informed her that he knew her decision was based on greed. He drew attention to the size and location of her house, as well as the items and decor within it. He was not aware that it was thanks to her parents that she had such a property, but the lavish items inside it had all been purchased courtesy of big bonuses earned from the misery she had inflicted on countless unfortunate individuals. Roger almost broke into tears as he told her about how his dad had gone downhill, before asking her what she had to say in defence. This was a courtesy she had not expected, but he was a judge after all. He knew that nothing she said would make him feel better, but he had hoped, for the sake of his father's memory, to hear her say that she regretted her actions.

Linda was not ready to die, bound in a dining chair, in her own kitchen. She pleaded with Roger. She begged him to take into consideration that none of this was her fault and that he could put all this behind him if he just walked away. Her loathing for the man was too evident in her patronising tone. He questioned if she thought him to be a fool. Linda then lost what little resolve she had been maintaining and let loose her tongue, in a fountain of venom towards both Roger and his father. Her nostrils flared, her eyes narrowed and her rodent-like features were highlighted as she spat out her insults.

"You think you can get away with this? Any of it? Shit

like you will rot in prison. You think you're important here – think you're some sort of judge? You're old and past it. You'll die just like your stupid father. Maybe if he had put a shift in once in a while, instead of trying to sponge off the system, he wouldn't have died such a pathetic death!"

That last addition proved a big mistake, as the judge rooted through his toolbox, his eyes and hands searching for the appropriate tool in a maniacal fashion. He glided towards her with a Stanley knife in a movement that seemed too chilling to be anything other than supernatural.

"I don't intend on going to prison, love. I'm signing out after this. I'll likely be off to hell, but I'll be sending a prime candidate for the unforgiving pits of Hades there first!"

He grasped her right ear with a vice-like grip as he proceeded to hack away at the cartilage connecting it to her head. Linda writhed wildly as she endured the unbearable pain of a corroded blade slicing through her tissue. It felt like fire, red hot. Roger shouted above her yells in laboured grunts.

"You don't seem... to have been... listening... to me."

Even in the centre of the red mist which had descended upon Roger, he still found space in his mind to recall the tale of how Saint Peter had cut the ear off of one of the soldiers arresting Christ in the Garden of Gethsemane. On this occasion, Christ would not be there to resolve the issue. As far as Roger was concerned, this bitch was for Satan to deal with.

A pain then surged through him, interrupting his cutting. The defendant had sunk her teeth into his left forearm with a terrier-like bite. He tried to pull away, but she would not relinquish her lock. This was her only chance of fighting back. Roger still had his fist around her ear, which was hanging on by a thread. He was not about to be beaten at this late stage, and in a move that was nothing short of agonising, he yanked away his arm as his skin was torn apart by the remaining teeth of his defendant. At the same time, the chunk of flesh that had belonged to his body less than a few seconds earlier went flying. Linda yet again cried out. She was still suffering the searing pain of her ear having been removed from her head as well as the impromptu tooth extraction.

Roger grasped his arm. A volcano of blood erupted from the gaping wound. Linda began bucking in the chair, wishing she had not insisted that Mick buy the high quality kitchen table and chairs over the cheaper, mdf seating implements. They would have easily fallen apart with the force that she was putting into escaping but she had insisted on quality; never envisaging that she would one day be in a situation like this, not even in her wildest dreams. She threw herself to the left, and the entire chair went down. The legs were damaged, but it remained intact. The damage had given her a sliver of room to break free. She proceeded to wriggle, like an invertebrate frantically attempting to escape the peril of an oncoming shoe, until she felt a meaty hand reach down and once again seize her hair.

"You're in my courtroom. You're on trial for murder

and you will confess, you stupid bitch!"

Roger was losing his composure. His face had become as red as a tomato. In any other situation it would have been comical.

"Get off me, you freak!"

The bite had really hurt Roger. He was losing a lot of blood. In the week leading up to his final courtroom appearance, the rate that he had been drinking – and the illness he had suffered as a result of it – had caused him considerable damage beneath the surface. He began to worry that he may not be able to finish his career as a judge that night. That thought fuelled him enough to keep going, even though he felt like he could collapse at any moment. He dragged the defendant by the hair once again and tried to raise her back to a seated position, so that she would be facing him again. The legs of the chair were no longer stable. It crashed to the floor, falling apart.

Still strapped to the remnants of the wooden structure, but now lying on the floor, Linda started laughing. It was a manic and crazed laughter, given the fact that she was lying next to her severed ear. Her cackling only made Roger more irate. He dropped to the floor, straddling above the wreck of the chair and the woman responsible for his father's death. In an innovative attempt at defence, Linda took advantage of the judge's position and wrapped her legs around her aggressor as tightly as she could. He, at the same time, wrapped his hands around her throat. She laughed again. Her bruised face, combined with missing teeth and a severed ear, made her look truly monstrous as she cackled away and taunted Roger.

"You gonna try and shag me, old timer?"

She enjoyed seeing his frustration but did not realise that angering him further just made him more powerful, preventing any chance of a possible escape.

"You killed my father. You are responsible for his death. You above all started this – and you will pay with your life!"

Linda could squeeze tightly with her legs – but not enough to cause the same damage that Roger was causing to her with his strong hands around her throat, both thumbs pressing heavily upon her windpipe. His face began to redden tremendously; hers began to turn blue. Roger felt a trembling inside him. It was increasing at an alarming rate into a crippling pain, stealing his breath. The defendant's legs had lost their strength as the life drifted out of her body. Roger felt something seriously wrong with his internal mechanics. Linda began to gasp for air. She choked like a fish out of water, unable to provide to her lungs the very air she needed to live. Her vision became blurred as she looked up at the man who was in the process of killing her. His eyes were bulging. His face was completely crimson. His grip lessened ever so slightly. Roger felt his strength waver. A fire burned deep inside his chest. The furnace was becoming hotter and hotter, sending his system into overdrive. His vision began to go in and out of focus amid black flashes. He knew something very bad was going on. He had to finish his work. Failure was not an option.

Linda sucked in air like it was escaping into a vacuum in space. The hands suddenly loosened their grip entirely on her throat. They departed it altogether. Her relief was short lived. They moved to her shoulders and began to beat her torso repeatedly against the hard kitchen floor tiles. The judge was screaming at the top of his lungs.

"You killed me dad – you bitch, you killed him – you evil sack of shite."

Blood gushed from behind Linda's head. The slamming became milder. She had passed out from the pain. Before she had, a good chunk of her mind knew that she would be unlikely to wake up again. Her killer would likely carry on until there was nothing left of her.

The slamming did carry on, but soon it gave way to exhaustion. Roger felt like his chest and head were going to explode. He knew enough about health to know that he was almost definitely having a heart attack. Coronary problems ran in his family, and it had been a heart attack that saw his dad end up in hospital in the end. The stress of a ruined life. Roger felt like he was going to experience the same fate. He was blacking out and knew that it was the end. Looking at the bloodied and mutilated body beneath him, Roger felt content that his work was done. His dad was avenged. In his death throes, he made sure to fall backwards. He was not about to die lying next to the bastard that had ruined the lives of two Birches. He gazed up at the ceiling. The strip light in the kitchen flickered and flashed. The starter needed changing. He had heard many a film joke about walking towards the light. He was too tired for that. He never went in for what he regarded as superstitious hokum anyway. He closed his eyes for what he believed would be the final time and spoke a final few words – half to himself, half to his dad.

"I got there in the end. I finally managed it, Dad. See you soon."

TWENTY THREE

A yellowed-magnolia ceiling stretched out to meet avocado-and-cream wallpaper. There was a smell of bacon, or some variant of frying meat, in the air. The house was spotless, even the green carpet, despite there only being an old carpet sweeper in the room. A kettle whistled upon a nearby hob. A middle-aged man, with greying black hair, could be seen through the doorway, taking the kettle off the stove and extinguishing the hob.

Roger lay on a sofa, looking at his hands in disbelief as to exactly where he was – how he had ended up in his childhood home. *Is this death?* His mind forgot the pondering in an instant as he sat up from the sofa and looked around at his father's apartment – the one he had lived in for most of his childhood.

"You're up then, are you? Fancy a cuppa old son? You look like you need it after that skinful you had last night."

"Dad – Is that you?"

"Bloody hell, son. What were you drinking last night – anti-freeze? Of course it's me!" Billy laughed; Roger looked totally bemused. His dad walked off into the kitchen as Roger wheeled his legs around to touch the floor. Bare feet sank into the carpet. He clenched his toes. It felt real – warm and comforting, just like he remembered it. Billy came back in holding a plate, upon which were four rounds of bread with a hearty helping of bacon between each pair. There was also a mug full of tea. He placed them down. Roger went to sip the tea. He was desperately thirsty. Billy stopped him and placed two paracetamol down before him.

"Them first: they'll do you good. They'll go into your system quicker with a nice, hot drink."

Roger's head hurt like hell. His chest was tight, and he felt red hot. He trusted that paracetamol would be a good idea. His mind was trying its best to comprehend where he was and what had gone on. It was like a computer stuck in an endless boot sequence: he simply could not focus, but he knew something was off. *This can't be real.*

Billy entered the room and turned on the television. It was BBC, but the picture was cloudy and mainly white noise. He cursed.

"Argh, me bloody race is on in a minute! Can you fix that, son? Do you know what's wrong with it?"

Roger tried to get to his feet. The sofa was very low, and he felt very sore. He failed the first time, but he managed on the second attempt. He shuffled over to the set and tried to read the dials, but the writing had worn off of them. He jostled the aerial. The entire room seemed to shake. Electricity ran through his entire system. He lost his balance and half-landed on the TV set. It was an old CRT unit with a wood veneer box surrounding it's circuitry, which served as a welcome perch for Roger.

"Careful, son – they're live wires behind there."

Roger wondered how an aerial cable could hold such a current. It had seared through his chest, which felt like it was burning. He tried to move the dials again, seeing if he could get some sort of picture. Ghostly shapes appeared amidst the white noise of the screen, but nothing definite came on. The aerial seemed to be in, and there was power going into the set. Roger tried the old trick of giving it a bash. Another wave surged through him, this time bringing him to his knees. He heard a strange voice, but there was only him and his dad in the room.

"Call it, there's no point, he's gone."

The lights in the room dimmed as though there were a lack of power. Roger called out in confusion.

"Dad?"

"Call the bloke, son. It's packed in again – bloody thing." Roger turned around and his dad was tuning in the radio. Commentary came on, but it did not sound like horse racing commentary. It was very medical. "I wish they'd stop putting these radio soaps on, who the hell listens to them?"

Roger felt ghastly. It was as though his mind was not working, not functioning as it was meant to. One minute, he was leaning over the TV unit – the next, he was sat on the sofa in front of the coffee table again. The situation made no sense, but Roger could not think about it.

"Are you going to eat that sarnie? Don't waste good meat. It costs a lot, that does!" Roger took a bite of his sandwich. It tasted good – as good as it always had back in the day – with extra butter on thick-sliced bread.

What day? How are we back here? Is this even real? Roger held his hands to the side of his head, applying pressure out of sheer frustration. He rose and moved closer to the radio, so that he could hear it better. It was not clear but it sounded like a very dramatic soap opera based in a hospital. As he ambled towards the radio, he carried the sandwich with him – chewing what was still in his mouth. The savoury flavour suddenly switched to an acrid dryness. His mouth lost all fluid and felt horrible, as though it was full of ashes.

"He's not responding." Roger's mind began darting everywhere as he fell to his knees in front of the radio and the dining room table it was on. He was a boy sat in a pram. He was riding his bike for the first time. He was starting the engine of his car for the first time. His first kiss. His first sexual experience. They all seemed to be merging into one. He tried to focus, he wanted to hear what was coming out of the radio. Everything seemed to be revolving around that one item.

"Just leave it, son. It's been acting up for ages, anyway. It could be dangerous. We'll get the man to fix it."

Roger's strength had left him, but he reached out with everything he had – aiming for the plastic knob on the front grill. As his fingers got within an inch of the dial, sparks began to fly from the old unit. It was malfunctioning and looked highly dangerous. Roger did not care about the danger. He had to figure out what was so important about the radio. His hand made contact with the unit, and he was flung across the room as Billy cried out.

"Son!"

Pain and shock seared through Roger's body as a bolt of lightning forked across the front of his vision. In one moment, everything was suddenly as clear as day. He saw the bright lights of a hospital room. He was lying on a bed. Doctors were all around him. One of them was holding what appeared to be two steam irons. His mind soon cottoned onto what they were: shock pads, attached to a defibrillator. *My heart must have stopped.* In the corner of the room was a man in police uniform.

Why is he here?

"I've got a pulse, I've got a pulse!" Blackness enveloped his vision as a horrible electronic sound filled the room. Roger could still hear.

"We're losing him again."

"Come on. We had him then."

"Clear!"

Roger felt his entire body tremble right through to the tips of his fingers and toes. The foreboding sound ceased to be an unbroken siren and became intermittent, sounding out in bleeps which formed a fragile yet steady pattern once again. His vision returned. Despite having wanted to die after his last case, Roger wanted to stay awake and enjoy every second of life in that moment, having been so close to death. He did not want to close his eyes again, but he could not help but squint at the brightness of the lights shining down upon him. He tried to sit up, but his body had no desire to listen to the mind. Time went by, and the personnel in the room decreased. A man in a white jacket holding a clipboard spoke to him.

"Looks like you won't be dying today, big fella. Time to get some rest."

A mask was placed across Roger's nose and mouth. Breathing felt easier: *Oxygen*.

Roger felt tired, more worn out than he had ever been before in his life. It reminded him of a romp with a girl he knew back in school. It drained everything he had, and he passed out virtually seconds after what had been a most divine ejaculation. There was no ejaculation this time, though it felt good to rest.

TWENTY FOUR

Linda had endured three weeks in Aintree University Hospital. She could not believe that she had survived the latest ordeal – a large part of her wished she had not. She had nightmares of her courtroom appearance every night, only to wake up in agony each time. They had tried to reattach her ear, but the skin refused to bond again: it was a horrible, jagged cut. Her face was disfigured from the damage it had incurred, and her head was half-shaved where they had needed to operate to prevent her cracked skull from putting pressure upon her brain. Soon after waking, she had asked for a mirror to see the extent of her injuries. The entire hospital endured her shrieking as she gazed upon the mutilated face staring back at her.

The head trauma that Linda's cranium endured had caused significant damage to her motor skills. She was unable to walk properly as a result of the shattered knee, which would require further surgery. She was denied a light at the end of the tunnel of her woes: doctors gave unanimously grave predictions regarding her recovery potential.

At first, she received several requests from news agencies requesting interviews. The second attempt on her life made her story worthy of national news, and the hype was further compounded by Roger's written confession-and-justification letter, which he had sent to several news outlets. One or two of the keener journalists actually managed to sneak into the ward. They were quickly sent away. One young girl managed to get a picture of Linda. That would likely provide her with a springboard to a great career, such was news. She was out of the building before Linda could do anything about it. She knew her picture would likely be plastered all over the internet that same evening. After that incident, she had told nurses to turn away anyone who was not family. She had none anyway – apart from Benny, who social services decided she should not see until she had healed up a bit more, so as not to shock him. Even then, it depended on whether or not he actually wanted to see his mother. She envisaged it was probably the latter.

Roger Birch had intended to kill Linda. In fact, he had caused her far more harm in life than he ever could in death. Even though she hated Mick, it was because of Roger's killing spree that the police were armed and ended up killing her husband. He may have endured a battering from unarmed police, but at least he would still be alive. She knew that, even if he hated her still, he would have came to visit her in hospital – if only out of loyalty as her husband.

Linda had always known that her job would come back to haunt her. She had always feared such an event occurring, but she had become complacent after years away from the position. Lying in a hospital bed had given her plenty of time to think, and she had been able to remember William Birch very well. He had been a victim of her attempts to keep her figures in the black. The old

Linda may have approved his claim, but the version of her that he had encountered was cold, callous and totally ruthless. She recalled how she had actually judged him the moment he and his son walked through the door. She saw him as one of those pleasant older men that everybody gets on with. The type who would look down upon her because she swore a lot. The type who would presume that she had got to where she was in her job by sleeping her way to the top. In truth, Billy did not care one bit about who she was, but she would never know that – not now that he was dead and buried.

She remembered the son – the big guy – but not as he was that day. She could only think of that monster dressed in black, whose face turned as red as the devil whilst he was literally choking the life out of her. She was not religious anymore, but Linda believed that Roger Birch was as close to Beelzebub as any human could be. One of the worst moments she experienced in the ward was when she had learned Satan was still walking the earth.

She had asked doctors and nurses repeatedly, but nobody would answer her questions regarding the condition of Roger Birch. When she first awoke, a nurse had informed her that Roger was alive. She had become hysterical. She ended up requiring considerable sedation. After that, nobody would tell her anything and she was forced to steal the newspapers of other patients. A good few of them had national publications, but she was grateful to find a copy of the Liverpool Echo every now and again. It seemed to follow the story more closely. Some of the main articles ranged from reviewing Roger's past to rehashing Linda's turbulent few weeks. She cried one day, when she read that a former co-worker had spoken to the paper. He had told the press that he thought that she was a total bitch and was surprised that nobody had sought vengeance sooner. She had thought that some people may have viewed her in a bad light, but seeing it in print was crippling. She had been foul to the former co-worker, and it was just another action she regretted – though the regret soon faded and turned to lament and hatred. Linda had always seen herself as the victim throughout her life. That would never change.

The most horrifying article of all was when she read that Roger was in the same hospital as her. It did not matter that he was in a coma: she was terrified that he may wake up and come to finish the job that he started. During a visit to check on her condition and take some notes on the incident, police had informed her that he was secured and being guarded 24 hours a day. That did not alleviate her fears at all. She wanted to get home, pack her bags and get as far away from Liverpool as possible – out of the country would have been preferable, Australia ideal. Such a venture was not possible. She could barely move without heavy medication for her pain. The doctors tried physiotherapy every now and again, but it was not proving successful. Her walk was more of a stagger, and the strength in her arms had diminished, making it difficult to hold onto things for balance.

As long as Roger lived, Linda knew she would never truly rest – she would never know peace. She had to know that the devil had left this world, but every newspaper she read each day did not bring her the obituary which she so desperately sought. Linda knew how the law worked: they would do their best to keep him alive. Doctors loved to study such patients. Ian Brady was still alive and kicking – Charles Manson, too. William Birch would be the next big thing to all the quacks in the world. He had to die, but she knew that the crippled, disfigured mannequin that she had been reduced to was incapable of ensuring any such thing. She made a silent vow in her head: she would put everything she had into regaining her mobility and making sure that Lucifer did not arise from his slumber. If she could get to wherever he was before he got to her, she *may* stand a chance.

TWENTY FIVE

Roger was unsure as to where he was or what, exactly, was going on. He would drift in and out of consciousness – always aware but never truly awake. He heard his condition discussed on many occasions by medical professionals going into great detail. Another voice rang out often. It did not use medical terms at all, but conversed with the nurses. It was not a voice he knew, and he presumed that it must be that of a policeman: the one he had seen as they shocked his heart back into rhythm. He knew what he had done. He could recall what had gone on. It had been Rogers's intention to depart the world after his final case. He truly thought that he would have done just that. The nuclear bomb inside his chest had gone off that night after he had brought about the demise of the harpy. He had wanted to avoid prison, yet there and then he felt like a prisoner in his own body – a series of drips keeping his mind confined solely within his head: an intravenous incarceration.

Some nurses came by the bed. They were blurry as Roger's eyes tried to focus on them. One changed his drips whilst another wrote on some paper by his feet. They made a few jokes between themselves. They talked about the football and recent happenings in Coronation Street. If he could have laughed, he would have; instead, he made an invisible smile within his head. An internal laugh of sorts. His whole life had been a soap opera since the moment he lost his father – a far more believable one than those which featured on British regional channels each night.

Roger had no intention of ending up in jail – he saw it as the ultimate injustice that he should suffer incarceration for avenging the death of his father. It would mean that those who had wronged his family had won, and there was no way he was going to let that happen. His head ached. He tried with all of his might to move, to see if it was indeed possible. His fingers and toes felt like they moved slightly, but he was not sure if he was just imagining it. He had no idea how long he had been there, no knowledge of how long his body had been out of use. He was able to think coherent thoughts, so he knew his mind was functioning, but a terrifying thought crept into his mind: maybe the connection between his body and mind was not as it should be. If his heart had stopped, which he was sure it had, then that would mean that no oxygen had got to his brain for some period of time, and it may well have caused him serious damage. Upon that insidious thought, he tried again – with as much effort as he could muster – to move his body. This time his fingers and toes clenched tighter. He felt it: it was no imagination.

During the time he spent conscious, in between some truly wretched dreams, Roger tried his minor exercises – when he was sure that nobody else was around. He was completely unaware of time. There was no window in his room, and the lights stayed on almost all day – only dimming at night. His movement increased, and he became able to slowly move his arms and legs, albeit without any great strength or force. It was an achievement, yet he still knew that the drugs being pumped into him were holding him back – ensuring that he remain bedridden and in a constant state of fatigue. He also knew that the moment the doctors would stop drugging him, the police would seize him like a hawk snatching a field mouse. They would be only too happy to hastily escort him to the court, before it hastily condemned him to a life in prison. *He* was the judge. *He* had passed sentences. There was no way that he was going to allow himself to end up behind bars.

Roger's body was becoming accustomed to the medication. Each time he found himself awake, his focus felt as though it had increased slightly, and he quickly became able to move his body with greater fluidity and dexterity. At one point, he even managed to fling his arm up to his chest. He had looked at his hand, the nails needed a good trim, he slowly closed a fist. It felt good, but that lagging feeling that comes with heavy sedation prevented him from doing what he really wanted: to push himself into an upright position. His forearm looked strange and had big stitches in it. He remembered exactly how that had happened: *the teeth of the hydra.* He looked around at the translucent bags that dangled above him. They were difficult to focus on, and they seemed to sway from side to side. At least one of them was keeping him sedated, and they all seemed to be attached to the one machine.

Roger sensed that nobody was in the room with him.

He was not sure if it was night or day – either way he had to take a chance. It was the first time he had managed to move his entire arm to such a degree, and he did not know when or if it would next be possible. He wiggled the fingers on his left hand slowly. He had made good progress with his digits. Reaching out with caution, he went to lean towards the machine that the drips were attached to, but the effort required to lift his torso to one side was too great. There was a red button, with writing next to it that he was unable to read. He was convinced that it could lead to his freedom. Concentrating and then counting to three in his head, he jerked his body over to the side of the bed. It hurt, and he saw a spike in the digital charts on the screen beside him, which he thought must have been monitoring his heart. Closer to the machine, he reached out his left arm and felt buttons – several of them. His fingers caressed each one, until they felt something larger than the rest. He tried to look, but the position he was in made the viewpoint impossible. Roger then took a gamble and pressed the button, holding it down for a good few seconds. It was far more of an effort than he imagined it could have been. The lights on the machine went out, and he drew his arm back to the bed so as not to arouse suspicion. *Always one step ahead.*

The lack of drips at first caused pain to surge through Roger's body. There were painkillers as well as sedatives going through the machine. He had not seen himself, so had no idea of the state which he was in, but he began to become more alert very quickly. Just as quickly, the morning nurses noticed that his machine was off – but put it down to nothing more than a technical fault and got it working again. The initial action proved to be all that Roger had needed: his vision became clearer, and he was able to focus on a flip clock above the door. He saw that it had just passed 10 and presumed that must be PM as the lighting appeared to be dimmer and there was a stillness about the ward which would not be the case were it AM. Roger shut the contraption off once again, just before the night nurse passed his door. He was tall, skinny and effeminate – but the best part of all for Roger was that the lanky individual was not very attentive. He just cast a perfunctory glance at the room as he passed every so often.

By the time morning had come, Roger had spent the entire evening trying to test his body to see what movement he was still capable of. He was surprised to find that he was able to move fairly well, but only at a very slow speed, and with considerable weakness. It was still an achievement, and it was a sign of significant progress made from a few days of tampering with his machine. The morning nurses arrived slightly earlier than normal, too early for Roger to turn the machine back on without his movement being noticed. His increased focus enabled him to hear the conversations a lot more clearly. One debate in particular provided him with some crucial information and his failure to switch the machine back on in time proved to be of great benefit. Two of the nurses had been arguing as to who was at fault for the machine being off yet again. It was their duty to ensure he was cared for appropriately but Roger's infamy was such that any mistake could put jobs at risk. An error which lead to his death would no doubt create a PR tsunami and heads would roll. The substantial NHS budget cuts of recent years meant that Roger's machine could not be replaced without taking one from another patient, one who was not suspected of multiple homicides.

"The guy's a murderer. We can't take one of the working machines off of someone who *really* needs one for the sake of this bastard. He's not going to *die* if it goes off for a few hours. He may be cabbaged anyway for all we know. We'll wait till the doctor comes on Tuesday. The stats have improved, and he'll probably want to look at waking him up."

That information set an imposing deadline for Roger. Once he was awake, he knew that he would have no hope of getting away. He was desperate to find out what day it was, and he was delighted when his eyes scanned the wall and realised that the flip clock also showed the day: it read 'Thu.' He had five days, more or less, to get out of there. The moment that the gathering of nurses in his private room ceased, he shuffled across his bed and held the red button down again. Even though it was daytime, he had to seize his opportunities when he could. Roger had no idea what he was going to do in the long run. All he knew was that he needed to escape before it was too late.

TWENTY SIX

Life itself is a market. Most people bargain for what they want, but some will resort to whatever means necessary to get that which they crave. Linda mused on that speculation she remembered from a staff meeting long ago. A man in a suit had tried to drive an insatiable hunger for great figures into her department over the course of a two-hour Powerpoint presentation.

Linda had given an interview to a supposedly-freelance journalist over the phone and provided them with an exclusive story. She hated doing it, and the young woman sounded excited and enthusiastic throughout the call. If she worked it right, she could make plenty of money from Linda's comments. Five minutes on the phone with the victim of two murder attempts could well make the ambitious young woman rich – or at least provide a solid foundation for a thriving career. Linda despised that she had needed to resort to such measures to get the information that she required, but the interview enabled her to find out that the so-called judge was in the same hospital as her: Aintree. It was technically in Fazakarley, but everyone referred to it as Aintree. He was in the same building, a few floors below, on Seaforth Ward. The journalist had said that he was heavily guarded – but a small doorway with a maximum of two police would pose more of a problem to a reporter with a large-lens camera and notepad than a fellow patient who may well be 'lost.' It was not the most cunning of plans, but it was all that Linda had given the state that she was in.

Linda was proud of herself for the way that she had handled the journalist. During the clandestine interview, which took place over the payphone in the corner of the day room, she had insisted that information on Roger be provided first – and that her request for it be kept off the record. The journalist had taken the gamble, knowing that Linda could have just hung up after she got what she wanted, but there was a part of Linda that wanted her story to be told to the world. She hoped that people would take pity on her. She did not entirely realise that such a story could be twisted in all manner of ways in order to ensure maximum print sales and page views. Whatever made the most shocking headlines would earn the most money. Sex, scandal, disaster: all are much sought after dishes on the news menu. Linda had been aware of some of the risks when she asked the nurses to stop turning away her calls, but her plan was a desperate one and left her with few options. The fact that she achieved her goal was one small pleasure she was able to enjoy in her handicapped state.

Linda hated the ward that she was in. She thought that the name of it alone was ridiculous enough: 'Cump-sty.' She shared her room with five other patients, all of which she viewed as 'half gone.' Her apparent poor quality of roommates would prove to be to her advantage. 'Fat old Ethel' in the bed nearest the door would defecate on her mattress most mornings, before going crazy as the nurses came to clean her up and change her clothing. The entire room would be permeated with the smell of raw faeces for at least 15 minutes before the nurses would notice, and on cue, Ethel's screaming would start as they commenced the clean-up process which took the efforts of the entire team on most occasions. For an old lady she was still very strong as she writhed and kicked. It was that daily incident which Linda intended to use to her advantage. As soon as she got a whiff of whatever emissions the toothless old hag had let loose, Linda would stagger her way to the toilet on her crutches and wait until the coast was clear. Then she would proceed out of Cumpsty Ward and make her way to Seaforth Ward, where she would endeavour to send Satan back to hell. She had no idea of how exactly she would do so, but she believed that a good idea would come to her during what felt like eternity sat in her hospital bed.

Whatever Linda decided to do, getting to another ward would be a struggle. She was not allowed to leave the ward or go walking alone. Her semi-paralysed legs were feeling less and less like they would recover with every step she took. The extent of the damage to her right knee was considerable, and she had to endeavour not to put any pressure on it. The left ankle still hurt from her battle with Mick. Still, she could just about hobble along, thanks to the crutches. She had managed to convince the doctors to allow her to visit the toilet unaided – a small slice of dignity in her shattered world.

After making the plan, Linda wanted to put it into action straight away. It simply could not wait. She awoke to disappointment the next morning. Withered old Ethel was gone, and the bed where she had lain remained freshly-made and empty. Linda cried. She could not think of another way of getting out of the ward easily. If her legs worked it would not be a problem, but the staggering wreck which she had become was incapable of anything other than a forced amble. She would be easily noticed before she got anywhere near the door. Her severe disappointment did not last more than a few hours, as the fat old lady was returned the same evening. The tires of the wheelchair she was brought back in were almost flattened by her immense weight. Linda mused over just how ridiculous it was that she was so happy to see an obese and incontinent dementia sufferer – her visit to court had certainly had a huge impact on her mind. She thought of Roger and imagined him smiling at the changes he had brought about in her life – the image sickened her. Linda closed her eyes that evening and knew the next morning was going to be a big one, she had to complete her mission lest she never again know peace of mind.

Morning arrived. Daylight flooded her room, and her zombified neighbours rose from their slumber. The usual appetising smell of breakfast filled the ward. Though Linda was hungry, she was hoping a certain less-appetising smell would soon arrive. She was not kept waiting long. 'Fat old Ethel' had barely finished having porridge shoved into her mouth by a brave nurse when she made a noise that was both loud and sounded very moist. Linda seized the moment and rose from her bed, grabbing her sticks. The stink was particularly foul, and getting out of bed had only drawn Linda closer to it. It made her want to gag, but she just kept moving. She did not even have to hide in the toilets as planned, because nobody took much notice of her. All the attention was being diverted to the then-screaming old beast who was bucking like a mule. Two young male nurses experienced great difficulty in restraining her; a third had the delightful job of scooping out the mess she had made and cleaning the region of her body which she had sullied.

Getting out of the ward after more than a fortnight felt amazing for Linda – a grand achievement in itself. The glass lined-corridor was a blessing to gaze upon. She wasted little time on the views of the surrounding garden areas, which were as full of cigarette butts as they were flowers, and hurried as best she could. The big sign by the lifts detailed the layout of the building, in order to ensure that no patient was ever unable to locate the department which they required. Her eyes scanned it rapidly. Adrenaline flowed through her veins. She eventually locked onto Seaforth Ward: seventh floor. To Linda, the sight of the dull gun-metal grey elevator door was heavenly. It would provide freedom from her current hell, and she pressed the button with ferocity when she got in front of it. The lift took its time, and she pressed it again several times – with all the patience of a toddler. A man, who was also waiting, gave her a strange look. She just returned a half smile, which looked all the more frightening due to her missing teeth. The man gave an uneasy look and focused on the closed elevator door. It was an act that would once have angered Linda. With things as they were, she was grateful: conversation would only draw attention.

Eventually, the lift arrived. The wait had felt like forever, as though it had stopped at each floor separately on the way there. She got in, and the man pressed lucky number seven. She indeed had luck that day. She still had no real plan. She had tried to think of TV programmes that she has seen, and the only thing that came to mind was pulling the plug on the man who had tried to kill her. She had presumed that he must be in a bad way, hooked up to some form of machine. Otherwise he would be in a prison infirmary, being cared for by their doctors. A sickening thought slithered through her innards like an insidious parasite, as she realised just how little she had thought her plan through, she felt physically nauseated. The man who believed himself to be a judge may not even be on any machines. Even if he was, there were backup batteries, alarms and vigilant nurses to think about. Any of those could prove a substantial hindrance, but it was too late to turn back.

"Num-ber, sev-en." The lift may well have been from the 1980s, the way it spoke. Maybe it was just overworked, worn out and waiting to exit its miserable life and enter silicon heaven. If it could talk more then Linda would have enjoyed the company. The short trip between floors had given her time to think, and thinking had allowed her nerves to get the better of her. The doors opened, and the blue and white colour of the NHS sign confirmed that she had arrived on the correct floor: *Seaforth Ward*.

Linda made her way down the corridor, knowing what she must do.

TWENTY SEVEN

Roger punched the mechanic, who staggered back slightly but then came back at him with a look that could kill. The scene could easily be mistaken for a wrestling gimmick, but Roger knew that he had thrown the hardest punch he could. This was one tough bastard. The mechanic seized Roger's shirt collar with a menacingly strong grip. The move restricted Roger's airway and held him in place as a powerful blow was dealt directly to his nose, blurring his world. Before he could gather his thoughts, a great white mass came charging at him that was unmistakable even to his blurred vision. The mechanic was fat and bald, and his milky-white head collided with Roger in the exact same place that the punch had landed. The grip was relinquished, leaving substantial creases in his shirt. Roger fell to the floor, clutching his nose, cupping both hands around the facial protrusion which had never previously felt crooked. The mechanic looked down at Roger with disgust.

"Now get the hell out of my workshop."

"You stole 600 quid from my dad." Roger replied nasally.

"If the old fool wanted to put a few extra bob in my pocket then that's his problem. Now get up and get up, and get out!"

"You bastard – you'll regret this."

"Go on, get back to that old relic you call a dad. See if he needs his nappy changing."

Roger's blood boiled as the mechanic walked away, laughing at the insult he had just made. He would not have the last laugh. Roger saw an old steel toolbox on a workbench and acted completely on impulse. Before he could even think, he had picked it up and clouted the mechanic around the head with it. The punch may not have caused much damage earlier, but the heavy steel toolbox certainly did. The stout, hairless man collapsed to the ground. The latch flew open upon collision, scattering tools and what looked to be a packet of cocaine everywhere. Roger then stood above the mechanic and grabbed him by the collar as had been done to him a moment ago. He hit him twice, just to make sure he did not spring back up for another attack.

"600 quid. Give me it, now." It was not the money – it was the principle.

"Will I hell, prick." The mechanic spat upwards: the spittle splatted against Roger's cheek. That was about all he could take. The wake of his father's death had not yet taken its full toll on him, and he was in a fragile state. Somewhere in his mind, he felt that if he could just get the money back then it would make things okay again – put everything to rights. He knew logically that such a thing was impossible, but the wonders of the mind are endless. He wiped the slimy, tobacco-brown saliva from his cheek and gripped the mechanic on his upper chest with both hands and began to slam him against the floor.

Depression had various stages. At that moment,

Roger was oblivious to any consequences that his actions may incur. He just continued slamming the fat, ugly man against the concrete in an ape-like rage. A loud crack echoed throughout the dilapidated garage. The attack method was born from a combination of temper, frustration and instinct. The fat torso was difficult to lift, but the immense weight made for greater impact as it came back down. He repeated the move until he heard a strange sound. He had never heard such before heard in his life, like a pile of eggs being dropped.

Roger was shocked as he noticed that the bald head was a different shape to the light bulb it had resembled just moments before. He gazed at his hands in disbelief, suddenly aware of what he had done. It was not that he had probably killed the man that bothered him as much as the consequences which may result from it. Roger rose again and looked down at the mess which lay on the floor. A small pool of dark crimson began to flow from behind the ugly, white head which had been made even more hideous by the assault. Roger noticed there was a bulge at the side of the man's overalls. He placed a shaking hand in the pocket and pulled out a roll of money: most of it 50s, some of it 20s. It must have been several thousand, but he was not about to stand there and count it all when somebody could walk in at any moment. He pocketed the cash and left the scene; there was nobody else left alive in the workshop.

Billy's usual garage had closed down. He had taken many of the different cars there that he had owned over the years, and they had never ripped him off. They even gave a free oil change once a year as a token of their appreciation of his loyalty. When his MOT test came up, he took it to a workshop he had seen advertised in the Liverpool Echo newspaper: Litherland Autos. It was a new business in an old and battered building. Following the annual obligatory inspection Billy found himself lumped with a bill of more than £600 – which he paid, leaving him considerably out of pocket. It was only after he had died that Roger was going through his father's papers and found the receipt for the work, written in scruffy handwriting without specification of exactly what work was completed. His dad's car was in good condition, and it was only major works that could cost that much. He had remembered his dad mentioning that the MOT had been costly, but he had not made a fuss about it. *Billy was like that.*

It was still early days after losing his father, and Roger was just easing out of the state of disbelief into a pit of bitterness and venom against all those who had wronged his old man. There were many figures floating around in Roger's mind, but in that moment it was the paper in front of him that flooded his head with the need to do something, to act in some way. Grief can have many various ill-effects on the mind of an individual – and as he looked at the receipt, Roger was convinced that if he could just right that particular wrong, then maybe his tragic situation could be made better. He knew it would not bring his dad back, but somewhere in the back of his mind it was as though he thought that it could. He had visited the garage with an unclear goal.

He had not actively intended to go looking for trouble, but deep within his subconscious he craved nothing more than the opportunity to exact some form of vengeance – something that would relieve the pressure release of the steam from the furnace his mind was building up.

In the days after the incident, Roger had fully expected to be arrested – at least for theft, probably for murder. He had spent much of his time sat in his apartment, drinking and waiting for the buzzer to ring: he would open the door and be greeted by Merseyside Police. Days went by, and it did not happen. The local news featured the story, and it seemed that the mechanic had many more likely enemies than the son of Billy Birch. Taking the entire bundle of notes had been a good idea, as police were viewing the crime as the result of a dispute between two rival drug dealers – especially with the cocaine left on the floor. Roger had only kept £600, the rest he had shoved through the letterbox of a small charity shop – one which always got overlooked when Government funds were being dished out. They may suspect it was dirty money, but they would accept it nevertheless: *better it go to something good.*

Roger had felt sick with worry as he imagined his impending police visit, but he did not regret that he had killed the man. It felt great to have finally retaliated, instead of just sitting there and accepting all the crap that had came his way. He had long been sick of living in a world where a thief can invade a property, but the owner who beats them up is the one who finds themselves under arrest – a world where a home owner will have to pay out of their own pocket to repair a window smashed by yobs, whilst the police try to befriend those who did it in an effort to aid so-called troubled youths – a world where the smallest hate crime takes precedence over all others, regardless of their severity. The events that killed his father had pushed him over the edge, and killing that mechanic was a step down a path from which he could never return. Roger knew this. He knew that even if he could get off the path, he would never want to.

People everywhere got away with so much. Decency had given way to greed. Politicians argued over which of the poor to point the national finger of blame at, whilst degenerate youths and remorseless bastards were running amok. *If they could get away with it, why shouldn't he?*

Roger was over 40, with no children and no partner in life. His father had been everything to him. He did not see himself as a hero, but he did see himself as the man who would make a stand and avenge his father. Roger had always loved vigilante films. The laws that govern real society can be bent, twisted and perverted so easily. The heroes in these films always played by their own rules. They got the job done. No ill-conceived law of the land would get in their way. Their actions had lived long in Roger's memory. They had inspired many an imagination throughout his life and the temptation to make such ideas a reality had been all to inviting whilst his mind languished in the dark of his depression following the loss of his dad.

The release that he had felt from that first kill had

been euphoric. He felt like he was making a difference, punishing the guilty party who had wronged his father – and almost certainly had wronged and would wrong others. Roger felt he owed it to his father – and society – to make a stand. He would not just sit back, take all the crap that he was dealt and say 'thank you' to the bastards of the world. If the law was broken then a true judge needed to castigate the guilty, and he was going to be the man to do it. He took a pen and began to write names down of those he believed needed bringing to justice.

Roger remembered how it all began with the utmost clarity: that first step down a dangerous path, which had ultimately led him to the hospital bed in which he was lying. He had never looked back. His dreams replayed his actions nightly, and he went through them all again whilst awake – an endless cycle.

TWENTY EIGHT

Linda made her way down the corridor towards Seaforth Ward. As she approached the double-doored entrance there were police standing in front of it – and other men in uniform, coming in and out. They were definitely not hospital staff. Her confusion seemed apparent to one of the door guards.

"Are you okay there? Where are you goi... hang on. Linda Painter? Wait right there."

Linda knew there was no point in trying to defend herself. She was disfigured, bruised and would be unable to get away at anything other than a snail's pace. She felt pathetic. Even her attempt at getting to the judge had been a joke: the way she looked drew attention to her. Anyone walking past her would have had their eyes drawn to the state of her face, and the police would know exactly who she was. The entire force would have been briefed on the Neo Ripper case. The officer guarding the door made a muttered speech into his radio that she could not make out, and within seconds a man in a long dark coat came through from the ward. He was dressed smart, with a shirt, tie and polished shoes – but the coat made him stand out. He enquired directly, abruptly and without emotion or introduction.

"Have you seen him? Did you encounter him?"

"W-who?"

"Look, I've not got time to play guessing games. The man who tried to kill you is walking free right now. Has he approached you, or have you seen him? Yes or no?"

Linda was taken aback and suddenly very frightened. She had thought that she could just about end a bed-ridden Roger given the state that she was in. If he was up and about then the odds of her managing such a feat had just lengthened considerably. The idea of *him* not only alive, but up and walking was as unimaginable as it was terrifying.

"No."

"Then why are you here? Something's going on and I want answers."

"I-I-I came to see him – I just wanted to see him."

"And *did* you?" The emphasis the man put on 'did' highlighted his abject lack of patience.

"N-no."

"Well, look. I'm DCI Jackson – call me Phil if you must. I've just sent men over to your ward to watch over you, and you weren't there. You could have been killed. You'll go back there with my officers now and stay there until we say otherwise – okay?" He dictated the conversation well, wasting minimal time.

Linda nodded as she was hastily escorted back to the elevator by two armed officers. She was forced to move as quickly as she could despite her condition and lack of mobility. The police were taking no chances. She was furious. Her one chance to finish the judge off, and she had left it too late. She lamented not having thought of her plan just a day earlier – then she would have been okay, safe. Instead, she was left completely powerless – like a crippled antelope hobbling away from a prowling lion.

She had the protection of Merseyside Police, but she knew just how cunning the man could be – he had remained anonymous throughout his murders. He could be hiding anywhere within the hospital, waiting to attack. It reminded her of a horror film she saw many years ago: Alien. Like Ripley with the Xenomorph, she did not feel that anybody could truly protect her from this monster. She hated him for the state that she was in; she hated his father for ever having come into her office and she hated most of all that Roger Birch – the Neo Ripper – was up and walking around somewhere when he should be dead. Her next course of action was unclear, but she knew that she needed to think of one quickly if she placed any value at all on her life.

TWENTY NINE

Roger almost laughed at how easy his escape had been.

★ ★ ★

It had still been dark in his room, and the lights in the ward were dimmed. The sleeve of a high-visibility jacket could be seen hung from the back of a chair just outside the door of his room. No nurses had been around, the ward was silent. Roger had tested his limbs and felt that he could move them all – not greatly, but the drugs he had been getting pumped with had started to wear off. He had tampered with his machine at every available opportunity. The movement was a blessing, but with it came great pain. He had looked down his chest one night and saw a huge gash held together by a series of heavy duty stitches: *heart surgery*. The former judge knew that he was not going to get far in the state he was in. In truth, all he wanted was to get away and die on his own in peace. He was the law, and judgement would not be passed upon him – *not in this life anyway*.

He eased a leg over to the side of the bed and then another. He was clad in hospital pyjamas and felt pleased that it was not a gown – he did not want to look ridiculous with his buttocks on display if it all went wrong: he still had his dignity. His feet met the cold tiles and sent a sensation through his body as he remained sat upon the edge of the bed. He removed the needle from his arm, which had been delivering the drips to his veins when the machine was working. It bled but not too badly. Time grew short, and he knew that he had to move. The big test of standing up was coming. He did not know how he would fare, as he was unaware of the date or how long he had actually been on that bed. The flip clock in his room had made him aware of the time and day but not the date. He knew that muscles could deteriorate if left inactive for long periods, but as he made an attempt to rise, he managed it with only a minor struggle. He felt weak, but that was only due to the lack of food in his system. A paste had been put down his throat at first via a tube up his nose, but that had been taken out due to complications. Only a few intravenous drips had provided him with minimal sustenance. Despite being medical professionals, the hospital staff had begrudged having to care for him, and they had only done so out of fear of losing their jobs. Fingers would be pointed if the killer had not gone to trial. Roger had wondered how many heads would roll for allowing his escape.

Taking his first tentative steps across the room, Roger's body soon recalled how to move about. He made sure to go slowly. His bare feet made no sound on the tiles, and he stared through the rectangular glass window in the door at the policeman outside, busy on his mobile phone. The officer had harboured no expectation that the sleeping Neo Ripper was going to wake up. He was busy on a website with pictures of various girls: a dating website. He knew that he had to get past the cop: there was only one way in and one way out of the room. Looking up, the flip clock showed 5:30, and Roger knew that he would need to act quickly before the majority of the hospital started waking up and commencing activities.

Roger saw himself as a judge, and he truly believed that he had never killed anyone who did not deserve it. Times were getting desperate. Searching the room, he found a pair of scissors and a scalpel next to a big packet of bandages. He thought for a moment as to whether suicide would be possible, but it had been such an effort to get out of the state that he was in that he did not want to risk his life being preserved again. There would be no chance of another such opportunity as that which he had been given. He looked again out of the window and the policeman appeared engrossed in his mobile phone, typing a long message to a girl who was pouting in her picture, which Roger thought looked ridiculous – *nobody smiles anymore.*

The smartphone screen shattered as it crashed to the floor, obscuring the picture of the pouting girl and leaving the message unfinished and unsent. Pain coursed through the cop's leg as metal entered his thigh. He looked down and saw both blades of a pair of scissors lodged within him. Blood stemmed steadily from the wound. He looked up and saw something far worse than any injury: the Neo Ripper stood before him, looking wrought and malnourished. The cop believed his life was finished there and then. Roger bent down in front of him as a small trail of blood oozed from the stitched wound where his heart had undergone surgery. The officer had both hands on his own wound as blood began to gush like a river from between the stainless steel blades. Roger threw a hand towel on the police officer's knees and spoke, which was more of an effort than he imagined it would be.

"The scissors have sliced through your artery. If you try and chase me now you will likely die from blood loss. If you stay put you can make a tourniquet and use your baton to keep the towel tight. Do this and you may just live to tell this tale." He pulled the police radio from the officer's vest. "Someone will come eventually. If you scream or shout, I will kill you. I don't want to do that, so don't force my hand. I'm sorry you had to be in the way. Are we clear?"

The officer had tried to speak, but in the end he just nodded. Roger walked off down the corridor. He was aware that his face may have been on the news, but he hoped that people would just see him as a wandering patient. Either way, he knew that he needed to get out of the hospital as soon as possible. He continued until he saw a sign for the main elevators to reception. His movement was slow compared to normal, and his body cried out for pain relief – *a Scotch would do nicely.* He pushed the elevator button and prayed that he would be able to make his bid for freedom before it was too late.

★ ★ ★

Roger had gone up two floors to radiology and found an open locker in one of the changing rooms. He helped himself to a set of tracksuit bottoms, a jacket and a base-

196

ball cap. Their owner was undergoing a CRT scan. Roger was sure to bin the bag so it looked like an outright robbery, not just a clothes robbery: that would only draw attention – *nobody robs clothes in this day and age.* It was not the best of disguises, but it would bring him less attention than hospital pyjamas and the cap would shade his face.

Roger knew that police would be expecting his escape from the building. They would be by all the exits and doors, and any attempt he might make to get out would result in his immediate capture. He was smarter than that, and relished in the fact that the police did not seem to realise just how intelligent and cunning he could be. Instead of escaping, he stayed in radiology. It was busy, and the main waiting room was packed with more than 100 people awaiting scans of some form. He picked a secluded spot in the corner where he could see a television which was showing the news. A photo of him appeared on the screen. It made him even more glad that there had been a cap in the locker. He had no idea where the photo had been obtained from, but it was an old one – *a lot less greys.* He laughed at the name they had given him. He had heard it before but never as a direct reference to him: the Neo Ripper. *Storms, celebrity couples – now me! They give names to everything these days.*

He felt the pockets of the tracksuit bottoms he had stolen, and there was change in them – he was grateful of that. He shuffled over to the vending machines and bought a bottle of Lucozade and a Pepperami. He was so hungry and thirsty that it seemed like a royal feast.

He sat back down and gazed at the television, careful to keep the peak of the cap lowered. His mini banquet may as well have turned to ashes in his mouth as a foul taste assaulted his tastebuds, and a discomfort spread through his chest. The television was muted and showing inconsistent subtitles, but the yellow ribbon at the bottom of the soundless screen claimed that Linda Painter was unharmed. A picture of her panned onto the screen. There was no mistaking it: *the bitch was alive.*

There was lots of talking among those waiting, and a panic started to set in before a member of staff came and changed the channel. Roger sat there shocked. He was sure that he had killed her. That was his final goal, and if she was still alive it changed everything. He had been considering accessing the roof of the hospital and taking a dive off the tall building, but he could not contemplate such an act without finishing what he started. What made it even harder was that he knew that she would now be heavily guarded, and he doubted that he could manage it in his weakened state. She had been judged and sentenced to death. He was retired. This was not meant to be. Roger knew that his heart was not in a good state. It felt worse with this news and worse still as he tried to find a way around it all in his mind. He did not even know where she was, until fate gave him a helping hand.

A man stood on a seat and pushed the buttons on the bottom of the wall-mounted television which got the news back on. Those in the waiting room had kicked off quite a fuss at the channel change, and it was obviously too much for them not to be able to follow it. Given that they were in the very hospital where the events were unfolding, it was understandable. Staff had tried to maintain calm by not allowing them to see it, but it was a pointless endeavour in an age where almost everyone had access to an endless library of information in the palm of their hand. Changing the channel only made the mood in the waiting room even more tense. The point where the news had come back on was showing a path which Linda would have taken to get to Roger's ward. It was mainly filler: it was obvious that the police had released little information for the press to work with. The press had gone ahead with it anyway – dragging it out and getting a few psychological experts on in between. Roger thought it was funny that Linda had attempted to get to him, and even funnier that he had been gone a good while when she had. He loved the idea of her being angry: with the pain she had caused his father, she deserved it.

When detailing Linda's path, the news gave away Linda's location. They had likely not expected Roger to be sat comfortably watching the broadcast. Cumpsty Ward was to be his goal. Roger had no idea how he would get past police, but he thought that he would think of it along the way. He put his faith in his mind. Time was running short, and he needed to act. There was not even a guarantee that she would be there, but Roger knew that she would be in quite a state after her appearance in court. He trusted his intuition that she would indeed be there. It had not let him down throughout his time as a judge. Waiting would make no difference, and rash actions would not help him ensure that his final judgement was upheld. There was a young lad sat opposite him who smelled of cannabis. He had to take a chance.

"Ay lad, how far is that from here?"

"I think it's the 11th floor, mate. A load of bizzies got in the lift there when I was on me way up. I thought they were after me stash, but their boss pressed 11!" The young man spoke with a schoolboy's glee at evading police attention. Little did he realise that the last thing on officer's minds now was a youth carrying a small amount of cannabis. It was all the information that Roger needed. He chuckled along with the lad whilst devising at what point he would make his way to the 11th floor. Whilst Roger waited he carried on following the news, which was showing a path which police believed he might have taken in his escape from the hospital. He was glad that they did not know much about him. Either his letter had not been printed, or police had not taken it in properly. It explained his reasons for each killing and spoke in detail about his ultimate goal: to achieve vengeance for his father. Anyone who had read that would know that there was no way he would flee when his final mission was still incomplete. Whatever the case, police did not understand his motives, and he hoped that fact would be the difference maker.

THIRTY

Linda lay in her bed as police circulated the ward to the soundtrack of static-rich radio chatter. From what she could gather, they believed that Roger had fled and gone into hiding. She heard one doctor speculate amongst some of his fellow staff that he believed the Neo Ripper would not last long, his condition he was most dire. She was not allowed to watch television: none of the patients in Cumpsty Ward were permitted the news on. The aim was to avoid widespread panic, but it proved ineffective as visitors passed information on to their friends and relatives and those with mobile phones easily stayed in the loop whilst those without picked up on what gossip they could. Relatives visiting their families gave Linda dirty looks as though the situation was her fault. Their visiting hours were restricted, and getting into the ward took forever due to the heavy police presence. It sickened Linda, and she imagined Roger once again telling her how it really did all boil down to her – just like he had done on that fateful night. She was filled with malice towards both him and his father.

Hours had passed, and the police patrols soon died down. They aimed to concentrate numbers on where they expected Roger to be. Linda heard Walton being mentioned a lot, but none of the officers gave her much information. After what felt like an eternity of being ignored, a man came and gave her an update. He was fat with a jolly face and a belly that hung over his waist line. As pleasant as he was, Linda scoffed at the idea that a man in his state could be a police officer. She was finding that she had nothing within her but venom and contempt for the vast majority of people since she survived her run in with Roger – even those who were nice to her. The officer told her that Roger was not believed to be in the area, and that they were doing all they could to track him down. This information filled her with minimal confidence.

The day dragged on as the sun descended into the horizon, and the bright fluorescent lights of the ward appeared even brighter as the gloom of dusk took over. The police radios were still active, but less so than earlier, as were the patrols within her ward. Linda was sat up in her bed on a slight incline. She was dog tired but doing her best to remain awake. She had to know what was going on. She had tried to call out several times, but she kept getting ignored or told to calm down by nurses. Her eyes began to shut until she saw a high-vis jacket from between the thin slit between her eyelids as she fought to remain conscious. She called out and, on this occasion, the officer came over. She asked for an update and told them she was frightened and unable to sleep due to the lack of information. The officer told her that his boss would clarify the situation in a moment. The clock read 19:55, and most of the ward was largely silent as it had been since the evening meal was served. Linda was amazed that nobody else in the ward seemed to share her fear. She wondered whether they were all part of some conspiracy for her to be finished off. She narrowed her eyes in hatred, and thought of how she loathed them all.

Eventually, DCI Jackson showed up and gave her an update. "Okay Linda. We have scoured the hospital and are more than certain that Roger Birch is not in the building. He's not in good health and the doctors who were dealing with him have told me that it's unlikely that he'll last the night without medical aid. We've got every man available scanning the immediate area right now. He will be found and dealt with before morning. I'll leave an officer stationed at the ward entrance, and hospital security are at hand should they be needed. If a problem arises, my men can be here within an instant. Any relevant news, we will inform you. Now get some rest."

The DCI was so brief and blunt, Linda could not believe it – it was as though it were a pre-rehearsed statement. She had not had chance to speak a word back to him before he turned and left the ward, his long black coat waving behind him. As much as she hated the state that she was in, she had hoped that it would get her some nicer treatment – some TLC – but ended up feeling like people harboured as much ill will towards her as they did the Neo Ripper. She had read a few newspaper articles which had painted her in a not-so-innocent light. Several of the tabloids had focused on her old job and she presumed that many people must have formed their opinions based on them. Laying on her hospital bed, a prisoner in her own body, she imagined herself living out her days in some home, having her arse wiped and staggering to the communal gardens once in a blue moon. Her parents were long gone, and she had lost what few friends she had through being a renowned gossip. She lamented not having been a nicer person in life, even musing that she would likely not be in the situation which she was in at that moment if she had just remained the woman that she had been when she started the assessor job. It was all too late for that. Even her own son hated her now. She tried to convince herself that it was for his benefit that she had put everything into her job and had become who she was, but she knew deep down that she had got off on the power and the wages that came with it. Linda sobbed, and tears ran down her bruised cheeks as she drifted into sleep.

THIRTY ONE

The chaotic queues in the radiology department were something Roger was most grateful for. He had sat hunched with his head lowered for several hours, watching the news in the packed waiting room. The clothes he had stolen helped him blend in seamlessly. Most people there had been waiting hours for their appointments, so the length of time he had spent there went completely unnoticed. At one point, he thought that his cover was blown. An old man seemed to stare at him as though consumed by déjà-vu, but Roger soon realised that it was due to the fact that there was a clock on the wall above where he was sat. Though the news caused a stir, most people were more concerned with the delay in their appointments. Time drew on, and the room slowly emptied. Roger knew he would have to act soon. He felt awful. Though one of the drips had been sedating him, the others filled him with painkillers, and he really would have liked some of them. His chest was very sore where the wound, which still oozed slightly, was located – and he had an awful migraine headache.

The news had given him almost all of the information that he needed. It eventually provided a follow-up, stating that police had received reports that he had made his way up to Walton and had been seen there. Grainy security footage showed a figure like him stood at the counter of a convenience store buying a bottle of some spirit. Even Roger thought that it was a little quite the doppelganger, and predicted that the poor guy was going to be in for quite a shock when police caught up with him. He knew it was only a matter of time before this happened and that he had to make his move before it did. Upon that thought, he made his way back to the elevator. He would head for the 11th floor and pay a visit to the wicked witch in Cumpsty Ward. He thought it was a ridiculous name for a hospital ward, but he remembered a road somewhere nearby named that and presumed it to be a local, of some importance, from the past. The number of police that he had seen on the screen in Walton had filled him with a little more confidence about finishing what he had started. There would be very few who would think he may still actually be in the hospital. His strength was wavering, and he felt sick to his stomach. He had not died during his final courtroom appearance, but he knew that the reaper was very close in Aintree University Hospital. He would welcome him, embrace the cloaked, scythe-wielding skeleton – but not before he had completed one final task.

The short trip up in the lift made Roger think of the guillotine, and that thought lead him on to consider his position as a judge. He had held onto that thought throughout his quest for vengeance, but technically he had retired from that profession. If anything, he regarded himself as an executioner at that moment. In what would be his final role on earth, he had to ensure that the sentence was carried out. Having passed it as a judge was not enough to ensure that justice was served. The elevator doors opened, and the robotic voice ensured him that he was on the correct floor. He followed the signs and was delighted to see one solitary policeman stood in front of the double doors which led to the ward. He hoped there were not more within. Roger kept his head lowered and walked with his hands in his pockets. He looked like any standard male from the surrounding areas, and there were a few people in the corridor – mainly hospital staff. He had actually thought that he might get through the doors without a problem, but that was asking too much. As he neared, the sentinel made a cold statement.

"Visiting hours are over."

"I'm just going to see my Dad." *Hopefully.*

"Sir, there is a strict security procedure in operation whilst…" The officer on the door stopped his sentence as he recognised the face of the man he hoped he would never have to see. He reached for his holstered taser gun, but the fastener prevented him from drawing it before Roger Birch could jab him in the throat. Roger did not have much strength in him so had made best use of strategy. There was no way he would be able to do any harm through an armoured vest. *Maybe a few years ago.*

The officer clutched at his neck, gasping like a fish out of water, seemingly unable to breathe. Roger knew that the guard would be okay. He had a surgical knife, which he had picked up from the room where he had lain bed-bound for weeks. He could have used it, but he was not about to sentence a man without trial. He did enact a fail-safe measure, by withdrawing the taser gun and shooting the officer with it in the leg. He shook and spasmed on the floor. Roger would have felt bad about it if he had the time to think, but he had one goal in mind: it needed to be completed, before his final chance to do so expired along with what life he had left in him. He walked into the ward, and within seconds he heard a scream from behind him. Somebody had found the police officer already. This shortened his window of opportunity even further. He drew the scalpel in front of the reception desk as three nurses, two in blue one in green, gazed at him in horror.

"Where is the bitch?" Roger barked, confident they would know exactly who he meant. They went into a fit of incoherent stammering.

"I'll ask again. Linda Painter – where is she? God almighty. Do not make me ask a third time."

"F-f, room f-four."

A feeble gesture was made to point in the direction. The nurses were unaware that Roger had no intention of killing them. As soon as he made his way in the direction they had told him, he heard screams and frantic footfall behind him. Roger had watched many a film in his time and found it funny that there he was, a supposed killer on the loose, raising hell in a hospital. In the split second that the thought entered his head, he pondered as to whether a film would be made about him, perhaps a book written. He hoped they would portray him in a good light: everyone loved Walter White, after all – and he was making life-destroying drugs for a living. He saw the plastic sign affixed to a wall above a set of double doors for room four. He gazed through the glass at the large room which contained six beds. Almost all of them had the curtains drawn around them, making his search more tedious. The former-judge-turned-executioner made his way into the room. He would finish what he started. *It ends. One way or another, it will end.*

THIRTY TWO

Linda had heard shouting, running and then screams. There was no doubt in her mind as to why they were occurring: the lunatic had returned, and his demonic presence was striking fear into the hearts of everyone. Nobody realised that it was only her that he was after. She looked on in fright as the tall presence entered the room. He was her own personal doom, personified into a monstrous form. Dead eyes scanned the area, searching for her: his victim. Linda closed her own eyes for a moment, in the hope that he would just disappear. This could be another of her terrifying dreams that she had been having since Mick had attacked her. She opened them again and realised that it was no dream. This was real. The devil had come for her. There he stood, in a designer-brand tracksuit he had likely stolen, looking much worse than the last time she had seen him. He was unkempt. His face was as pale as the moon. He began pulling the curtains back on the beds. Concerned patients gazed upon his presence in terror and wonder. Several of them were banking on him only being there for Linda and leaving them alone. One of them screamed as Roger thrust the curtain back; he just carried on scanning the room like a machine.

All had fallen quiet as a terrifying stillness rented the silent air. There was only one bed left: hers. Linda knew that she had to act first were she to have any chance of surviving this hell. Roger took in a deep breath and drew the final curtain back almost calmly with his left hand. The scalpel was in his right hand, ready to end the bloody trail which his life had taken. Linda was not there. Before he had time to think, a half-crippled woman had galloped across the room. She struck him across the head and back with a walking frame, using every ounce of strength that she had in her body. The remaining effects of the sedative drips and Roger's weakened state had affected him more than he had expected. He usually had razor-sharp senses. The executioner staggered to one knee. He flailed out with the knife, but slashed only air. Linda again raised the Zimmer frame. She struck Roger once more. He groaned and was reduced from a kneeling position to all-fours, propping himself up with his arms but losing his grip on the surgical steel weapon. Linda tried to raise her makeshift weapon yet again, but her strength was almost depleted. She was much slower on the third attempt.

That was all the opportunity that Roger needed. He lunged himself forward in a rugby tackle attack. It floored Linda; the frame clattered to the floor. Had Linda summoned the strength for one last strike with it, she may have been okay. Roger pinned her down. The onlooking crowd of patients all gasped as he gained the advantage – apart from one who remained asleep. Roger was annoyed at himself for having been fooled. Linda was mortified that her surprise attack had not worked as she had hoped. She was lucky to have been in the visitor toilet when Roger arrived. She would normally have used the patients' one in the room, but fat old Ethel had not long been taken there by her family during visiting hours. Linda had not been keen on using the same lavatory so soon afterwards – the obese OAP had been in there a long time.

Her attack had helped her a little. She fought against her weakened executioner, who did literally look like death – he was so pale, and his eyes were so heavy, that he could have easily been mistaken for a zombie. Roger felt the pain as she scratched and clawed at his face, but adrenaline was flowing through his body. He was adamant that nothing would stop him this time. What was beneath him looked foul, battered and bruised. It was also missing several teeth, as well as an ear. He thought his final act upon this earth would be doing her a favour – putting her out of her misery. Her arms kept raising, and he did not have the strength to restrain her like he had during their previous encounter. Linda was fighting with the resilience of a cornered rat. She even tried to rise up and bite Roger with what teeth she had left. It had worked well last time. She almost caught his arm with the move, but once again, she left herself defenceless. Roger dodged the bite and gave her already-broken nose a strong headbutt – causing a river of blood to immediately gush down her upper lip as a terrible pain surged through her head.

Linda was convinced she had lost, until she saw blood that could not have been hers upon the jacket of her aggressor: an oval patch, which looked sodden. She desperately tried to slip a hand free and managed to do so, despite Roger's best efforts to keep her down. Linda threw the best punch she could – which was difficult, given she was being pinned against the floor and had no decent leverage to put much force behind it. The blow landed where she wanted it to. Though it was weak, it caused Roger to lose his grip and groan in agony. He rolled to one side, amidst the oohing and aahing of the spectators. Somewhere nearby, somebody was frantically screaming "security," though whether it was a nurse or a patient was impossible to know. Linda tried to get to her feet, but the damage from their first encounter made a once simple task seem more like a mountain to climb.

Roger felt like his chest was going to blow open at any moment but was determined to complete his work. He picked up the surgical knife from the floor and dived at Linda, looking to land the killer blow. She had her back to him as she was trying both to crawl away and to get back on her feet. The knife pierced deep into the back of her thigh. It hurt even more as Roger drew it downwards, opening her skin like a zipper on a coat – one that he was adamant would not be fastened again. Blood pooled across the cream tiled floor, as Linda wailed from the both the pain and the knowledge that the injury inflicted would likely finish her. Roger yanked her backwards – an action that was made easier by the amount of blood upon the floor, which acted as lubricant. He thrust the knife downwards towards her back, but she rolled as he did so in an effort to avoid the lethal instrument. It punctured her right arm, and she cried out again. As a judge, Roger would have welcomed it, but he was not interested in torture this time. He had a job to finish. He was convinced that the reason he was still alive was because he was destined to complete his task as executioner, and he would be damned if anything was going to stop him. A meaty-yet-withered hand gripped Linda around the throat as she looked up at the man who was about to kill her. Despite her best efforts, she found herself in the same situation that she had been in her kitchen. Roger's eyes burned with hatred. His skin made him look like he had been exhumed, such was his complexion, and his teeth were bared like an animal.

The entire scuffle had not contained any dialogue until Roger spoke in a weary voice through gritted teeth. "You caused all of this, bitch. It's all on you. I'm your penance, and this – this here and now is for my dad. You'll not escape death a second time."

Roger pressed the blade to her throat, and was about to draw it across, when a voice echoed throughout the silent room, alleviating the tension temporarily.

"Roger, stop!"

Roger looked up. A man in a long black coat stood in the doorway to the room. Linda rolled her eyes backwards, but it made her feel sick. She knew the voice anyway: DCI Jackson.

"Whatever point you wanted to prove, you have. You've won, Roger. Just let her go, and let's talk – you and me. I can make sure you're looked after."

As the sentence was spoken, hospital security and armed police joined the DCI. He waved them back, but it was a futile gesture: Roger was not about to believe the nice guy act. He decided to reply, ensuring that he kept the knife as close as possible to Linda's throat without penetrating too many layers of skin.

"None of you get it, do you? The state of this sick society that we live in. Those who don't deserve help are given it whilst those who've worked hard all of their lives are left to rot. People are more concerned with political correctness than they are with making sure the people who fought for the freedom which we now enjoy are well looked after. This bitch below me: she started it all. She set my dad down a path to ruin – and for what? Figures? Statistics? Because the bastards in Westminster screwed up, the working man has to suffer – has to die. The whole country is corrupt, and no bastard wants to listen. I'm not alone, I'm just one of the few driven enough to act."

"Roger. Things can still be worked out. I'm sorry about your dad, I really am but if you kill that lady beneath you, then my men will be forced to shoot you. Is that really what your dad would want?"

Roger thought for a moment, taking deep breaths. He knew there would be no form of compromise with the law. He just wanted to make sure that he gave a decent response – one which may be the last sentence he ever spoke.

"None of you wanted to help my dad – it was you lot who finally finished him off, arresting a 62-year-old for assault on a man less than half his age. That about sums you up. You and that shower stood behind you. The law is broken and the world needed a real judge – at least I provided my dad's memory with some justice."

"Look, Roger. I'm telling you now, this is your final chance. Back off, let her live and you can live too, we can sort this out."

The DCI spoke with more gravel and seriousness in his voice. If Roger had wanted to live then maybe he would have considered listening and bargaining, but he knew deep down that the current state of play was well beyond all that. He had to finish it before the window of opportunity slammed shut. Linda had kept silent, clinging to the hope that the police would shoot her executioner before he had chance to act – as they had with Mick – but after the DCI's final warning she knew what was coming.

"I love you, dad."

The words came out in a second as Roger rapidly drew the knife across Linda's throat, ensuring that he cut deep enough to see her off: it went three inches deep and turned Linda's final scream into a stomach-turning gurgle. In the same moment, two bullets left the guns of armed officers and hit Roger in the chest, sending him backwards. He did not fall over straight away. His body sagged to one side, and then collided with the blood-soaked floor. Police immediately checked for a pulse on Linda and tried to hold the gaping wound on her throat closed. They ceased their efforts within moments: the excessive blood loss from her eight inch gash on the back of her thigh rendered them futile.

Fingers touched Roger's neck, but there was no pulse. One of the bullets had gone straight through his heart.

In the few seconds between the bullets penetrating his body and him taking his last breath, Roger's mind went through a whirlwind of thoughts. One of them was humour: the irony in the fact that his heart had metaphorically been gone since he scattered his dad's ashes across the Mersey, the final goodbye in this world. The other significant thought came as he lay on the deck whilst the organs within his body were shutting down rapidly. He gazed up at the bright lights on the hospital ceiling and thought how many people would likely see the end of his life as a defeat. They would claim that the Neo Ripper's killing spree had been brought to an end, that he had been defeated. In his dying mind, the only word that reverberated was 'victory.' He had won: his father was avenged, and he had completed his task in the end. He knew that few would realise his true motives. Even fewer would acknowledge that he was not a killer, but a judge whose only actions had been to punish the guilty. Most people would not understand him. They would not see things the way that he did, deeming him a vile murderer. He had never asked for life to go the way it did, and his quest for vengeance was not something he could have ignored. In a world plagued by self-obsession, Roger was one of the last of a fast-dying breed. With no wife or child, his dad had been everything to him – and his untimely death had been all too much to take.

Roger's eyelids descended as his tired eyes took in one last gaze of the world. His body was in awful condition, but he would not be needing it much longer. It had served its purpose, despite how he had punished it with vast amounts of alcohol during his time as a judge: *medicine*. The rest of him lay still, but the slightest of smiles crept across his face in his final moment.

He was walking into a pub; people were talking, and there was a happy atmosphere. His dad was stood at the bar collecting two pints of bitter. He looked around and smiled at his son. "Now that's good timing, I managed to get us a decent booth over there: crackin' view of the telly."

"Dad?" Roger asked with both wonder and disbelief in his voice.

"I know you've been mad busy with work but don't tell me you've forgotten who I am!" Billy laughed. "It should be a decent game today: Coleman's back in the squad, and that lot have got their third-choice keeper in goal. What score do you reckon?"

"Two nil?"

"If we're lucky, eh!"

Roger looked back at his dad and smiled, shaking his head slightly. He could not quite remember how he got to there, but a sense of relief had filled him as he met his dad in the pub. He was also unable to focus on the events which lead up to him arriving at the pub but felt like a long-standing stress had left him, despite having no idea of what it was. He sat trying to think and focus, he was not even sure which bar he was actually in but being there felt amazing.

He wondered what it was that was making him feel so great but before he could think any more on the matter, his dad gave him a jab in the side and pointed out that the match was kicking off. The referee blew the whistle and Roger shared a toast with his dad, both of them giving a hearty cheer as they did, a tradition they partook in prior to every game they watched together. Things felt better than they had for a long time. What had been wrong, Roger could not say but he would not waste a second longer thinking about it. *He was with his dad, and that was all that mattered.*

A small request

I sincerely hope that you've enjoyed reading *Judge*, my first novel.

In this modern era, it is increasingly difficult to stand out as a new author. Individual reviews are now more powerful than ever in encouraging people to purchase and read one's work.

I'd be most grateful if you could spread the word — that could be by telling your friends, or taking the time out to leave an online review for this book.

Your honest opinion will both help get my name known and help me improve for future titles. You can also follow me on Facebook using @SeanFCampbellauthor.

Sean F Campbell
Author
@SeanFCampbellauthor

Printed in Poland
by Amazon Fulfillment
Poland Sp. z o.o., Wrocław

53447531R00134